BILLY
(THE KID)

BILLY
(THE KID)

a novel

PETER MEECH

SENTIENT PUBLICATIONS

First Sentient Publications edition 2020
Copyright © 2020 by Peter Meech

Cover design by Kim Johansen, Black Dog Design, www.blackdogdesign.com
Book design by Timm Bryson, em em design

Library of Congress Cataloging-in-Publication Data

Names: Meech, Peter C., author.
Title: Billy (the Kid) / Peter Meech.
Description: Boulder, CO : Sentient Publications, LLC, 2020.
Identifiers: LCCN 2019033549 (print) | LCCN 2019033550 (ebook) | ISBN 9781591813026 (hardcover) | ISBN 9781591813033 (kindle edition)
Subjects: LCSH: Billy, the Kid—Fiction. | Pueblo (Colo.)—Fiction. | GSAFD: Alternative histories (Fiction) | Western stories.
Classification: LCC PS3613.E366 B55 2020 (print) | LCC PS3613.E366 (ebook) | DDC 813/.6—dc23
LC record available at https://lccn.loc.gov/2019033549
LC ebook record available at https://lccn.loc.gov/2019033550
Printed in the United States of America

10 9 8 7 6 5 4 3 2 1

SENTIENT PUBLICATIONS
A Limited Liability Company
PO Box 1851
Boulder, CO 80306
www.sentientpublications.com

For my mother, Carol Marianne Crockett,
who was born in Pueblo, Colorado,
and who loved the West.

ONE

Vibrating were the floorboards. Vibrating were the tables and chairs. Vibrating was the air. And before they could see it, they heard it—a freight train bawling its lonesomeness, and they turned their gaze to the rattling windows.

Boxcars rumbled past the cantina's windows, and a yellow head came bursting into view. The yellow head belonged to a boy who was not yet a teenager. His face flashed in one window, disappeared, flashed in another, and was gone.

The boy was running toward an open boxcar. He stumbled, nearly fell and shot ahead. As his fingers gripped the edge of the door, a hand from behind seized his shirt collar. The boy reared up on his heels and collapsed to the ground beside the boots of a railroad cop.

With his hand on the back of the boy's neck, the railroad cop marched the boy inside the cantina. Filling the doorway with his wide blue shoulders, the railroad cop asked in Spanish if any of them knew the boy, and the Mexican musicians shook their heads no. The railroad cop turned to leave, swiveling the boy around by the neck, and at that instant the band leader emerged from the kitchen, an open bottle of Coca-Cola in each hand. The band leader, who had blue eyes and who was not Mexican, shambled across the floorboards, favoring his right leg, and asked the boy if he was thirsty.

The boy took the bottle in his strong country hand and drank two large swallows, breathing through his nose. The band leader asked the boy where he lived, and the boy blinked his large brown eyes and lowered the bottle.

Trailer camp, the boy said.

What's your name, son?

Tommy.

Howdy, Tommy. My name's Billy.

Howdy.

I'll give you a lift home if Red says it's okay.

Billy threw a look to the railroad cop, and the railroad cop nodded his consent. Billy turned around to his band and said: *La práctica ha terminado*, and left the cantina with the boy.

Dust stirred into the air as Billy's Model T spun out from the cantina to the unpaved road. The dust had traveled here, to Pueblo, Colorado, on prairie winds from Oklahoma and Kansas, and now it was traveling once more, riding a hobo current of air and drifting through the open windows of Billy's car to settle on their clothes like powdered sugar. Formerly the dust had been the nourishing earth of flowing prairie grasses, and afterwards the life-giving topsoil of ten thousand wheat farms, but now it was just dust, plain unadulterated dust, blowing with indirection and indifference.

The car was built in '27, the last year of production. Billy had bought it as a retirement gift for himself, but went on working for some five more years. He had kept the car in good condition until this year, when the dusters rolled in. The dust had pocked tiny holes in the green paint and sooted the top halves of the headlights so many times they looked permanently half asleep. Inside the car the dust had seeded itself into the crevices of the seats and darkened the white striping to dun.

In silence they passed an unused rail yard and a hobo encampment, which was a piece of scrubland with a dozen men stretched out on the ground and sitting on crates, and they turned onto the blacktop, where they overtook an ice wagon. As the Model T rolled into town, Billy eyed his passenger askant. The boy's hair had congregated into clumps on his head.

Your hair is dirty, Billy said.

I like dirty hair.

Oh, you like dirty hair.

If I keep it dirty all the time, I don't have to wash it.

Billy nodded his head at the superior logic. And you don't like shampoo.

Pa says we can't afford any.

What about soap?

Same thing.

When's the last time you had a shower?

Week ago, trailer camp. A lady lent me her soap.

How long since your mother was around?

Died a year after I was born.

Lucky you still got your pa.

Don't like my pa.

Didn't like mine neither.

They fell silent again and Billy took the car into the center of town before he renewed the conversation.

Where were you fixin on goin with that freight, son?

New Mexico.

Would've taken you a spell. That freight was headed to Chicago.

Tommy's lips pulled back in a grin. His teeth were like dominoes falling out of a bag, all jumbled on top of each other.

That freight was goin to New Mexico, Tommy said. You can't fool me.

I wouldn't fool you, Tommy. So what were you fixin to do in New Mexico? Steal horses? Rustle some cattle? Or maybe just kill a man?

Tommy's eyes opened in surprise.

I was young once too, Billy said with a smile.

He wheeled the car past the red-brick buildings of Main Street, past the sidewalks dense with whites and Mexicans. Scattered among them were a few black-skinned men, some mestizos, a Navajo woman and two full-blooded Ute braves, whose land this once was and who always walked with the ghosts of their ancestors. All the men were booted up like cowboys, even the businessmen. And all wore hats against the sun. Only the cottonwood trees along the sidewalk braved the sun without cover, and their bravery was not inborn. It came from buckets of Arkansas River by way of the townsfolk, who looked upon the trees as their kin.

Billy slowed down behind the town's electric streetcar and pointed out a storefront shaded by a copper awning.

You been there yet, Tommy?

No, sir.

That's the Federal Bakery. Fresh doughnuts there four times a day. 6:00 a.m., 10:00 a.m., noon and 2:00 p.m.

Don't have enough money for a doughnut.

Don't have to buy none. People go there just to watch the doughnuts shoot out of the machine. Always a crowd at the window when it happens.

A hatless man in a worn jacket dashed across the street in front of Billy's car, and Tommy ducked down in his seat. Billy continued along the street and told Tommy it was all right, the man had gone inside Earl's Diner. Downshifting behind a slow-moving truck, Billy flicked his gaze at Tommy and asked casually who the man was. Tommy's response was to slope further down in his seat and chew his top lip.

Approaching the town's main stoplight, Billy pulled on the handbrake until the car rolled to a stop. Tommy drew his body upright and peered through the passenger window with furtive eyes. Flinging himself out the door the next moment, he disappeared into a crowd on the sidewalk. The stoplight turned green, and Billy pushed his foot on the spring-loaded pedal to engage low gear. All that was left of the momentary encounter between the two strangers was an empty bottle of Coca-Cola rocking on the floor and a slim paperback that had wedged itself into the crevice of the seat. Billy plucked the book out and brought it forward to his eyes. Part of the cover was missing, but the title was still legible— *Outlaws of the Wild West*. He turned the book over and read the breathless exclamation on the back—*Thousands of Hardcover Readers!* Spinning the wheel, he drew up to Earl's Diner and parked the car.

TWO

———

Leaning forward on his stool at the counter, Billy read the screaming headlines of *The Pueblo Chieftain*.

DROUGHT GETS WORSE!

A glass of water thumped beside his hand, staining the paper with two plops, and he upped his head. Rosa, in her freshly ironed uniform, planted her elbows on the opposite side of the counter and gazed at him with open affection. Underneath a tousle of dark curls were a pair of round dark eyes sparkling with mischief. Her name was the only ordinary part of her, Billy thought, and even the name itself had acquired a patina of beauty by the accident of her person. But he didn't covet the young woman any more than he coveted the juniper trees that timbered the foothills in their conical perfection.

Hola, guapo, Rosa said. Special's good today.

Special it is, then, Billy said.

Rosa swung her tousled curls and called out the order to the cook. When she turned back, her gaze traveled to the booth in the corner, and Billy followed it. Sequestered in the booth by himself was the same hatless man who had dashed across the street earlier.

His parched hair was the color of wheat, and digging across his tanned forehead was a trench of worry. His eyes were threaded with crimson, and the tip of his nose had pinkened with the sun. His hands were folded on the table, and Billy could see they were the weathered hands of a farmer.

Rosa, resting her chin in the chalice of her two hands, supplied the answer to Billy's questioning gaze. Come in two days ago, lookin for work.

She uprooted her elbows, twisted around to the food-out counter and twisted back with a thick china plate that she set on the paper placemat. Billy's eyes jumped over the fried pork chop and alighted on a foamy slice of white bread recumbent on the side of the plate. There was no crust, least not one he recognized, just a tan-colored afterthought that wound around the whiteness like a piece of parcel tape. Billy raised the bread to his mouth and took a hesitant bite.

This is tastin sweet, Rosa.

I know it. I give it to my kids for dessert.

What do they call it?

Wonder Bread. Comes sliced in the wrapper if you can believe it.

Rosa was twenty-three and had been married six years to the assistant druggist. The high school romance had never soured, and they had a five-year-old son and three-year-old daughter, both of whom listened to Billy when he told them to brush their teeth every night.

Seen the widow today? he said with a studied casualness.

Rosa wet the tip of a pencil between her lips and totted up the bill. Come in early this mornin. Asked about you.

Asked about me?

Wanted to know why you're always starin at her and never talkin to her.

Grace O'Bannion said that?

Rosa slapped the bill on the table and tossed her curls with a smile.

Billy took another bite of the Wonder Bread and let it dissolve in his mouth. Something about the texture—its insubstantial nature—reminded him of cotton candy. The first time he had eaten a piece of cotton candy was at the St. Louis World's Fair twenty-eight years ago. Only they didn't call it cotton candy back then, they called it fairy floss, and it came in a chipped-wood box, and it cost as much as a steak sandwich.

The bell above the entrance shook furiously. Most everyone who came into the diner Billy knew, but here was the second stranger in a day. The man who swaggered through the door had sleek dark looks and could have been the brother of Valentino. His suit was city-cut, with a fuller coat and wider stripes than any local tailor would inflict. His spats—unknown in Pueblo—were unusually clean and larger than they should have been. The man surveyed the room, the way a fire chief checks for exits and joined the farmer in the booth and laid his hat on the seat beside him.

Billy heard the sleek man introduce himself as Stokes, and Billy heard the farmer say his name was Frank in a cracking voice that sounded as if it had been unwatered for days. Because Stokes showed no desire to shake hands, Frank slid his off the table. As Stokes picked up a menu from behind the salt and pepper shakers, Billy could see Frank rub his palms back and forth on his knees, and he surmised the farmer was trying to rub away his anxiety.

Billy had scarcely come to this conclusion when Rosa rounded the counter with a pot of coffee. Angling her head in the direction of the two men, she said to Billy in an undertone: If I'm not back in five minutes, call the sheriff. Putting on her best afternoon smile, she sashayed over to the booth.

Coffee, gentlemen?

The men nodded.

Rosa flipped up their cups and tilted the spout of the pot. You gentlemen decide yet?

Out shot Stokes's hand to the level of her shoulder. Once we decide, we'll let you know, and you'll go get it. Make sense?

Sure, Rosa said with averted head.

Heading back to the counter, Rosa made a face at Billy that telegraphed her revulsion, and Billy relayed an understanding with his eyes.

Hey! You still servin breakfast? Stokes was elevating his voice for the whole diner to hear.

All the livelong day! Rosa said, spinning around on one foot and matching his volume and intensity to show she could not be intimidated. Waltzing over to the table, she turned her lips into a smile that was one notch below a grimace.

Frank lowered his eyes to his coffee cup and waited for Stokes to speak.

Eggs and bacon for both of us, Stokes said, sliding the menu behind the salt and pepper shakers. Eggs sunny side up, bit runny, not too loose. Bacon patted down with a clean dishcloth. I don't want no broken pieces, and I don't want grease enough to do the backstroke in. Think you can manage that?

If you like, I can bring over a big towel, and you can take turns moppin down the bacon yourselves. Her smile was still there, its wattage undimmed.

Stokes gripped his mouth. There was a clicking sound as he adjusted his two front teeth. With entranced eyes Rosa watched his thumb disappear as if swallowed by an ungoverned appetite. More clicking came, followed by a sucking sound. Embarrassed by her own curiosity, Rosa took a step backward, wheeled around and returned to the counter.

One more click, and Stokes spat out his thumb and said in a voice that was not a whisper: That's Pueblo charm for you.

Frank gave no reaction. He was pressing his hand on his stomach as if to quell a raging argument inside.

Five minutes later Rosa set the plates before them. Immediately Stokes salted and peppered his food with both hands. When he had seasoned the eggs and bacon to his exacting standards, he began eating. To eliminate any chance of digestive error, he masticated each bite slowly and with authority. Frank paced himself but finished early and found himself staring at a cooling piece of toast on Stokes's plate. With an effort he turned his eyes away.

My chauffeur tells me you spoke to him in the drugstore, Stokes said.

Frank's gaze flipped back. Yes, sir.

Where you from?

Oklahoma.

Farming man?

Was.

How long you been out here?

Week.

Our business is expandin. Need a man drive to Denver, pick up some merchandise, drive back.

Legal? Frank said in a whisper.

How's that?

Is it legal?

You read the paper much, Frank?

No, sir.

I'm a reader. Always have been. Newspapers, magazines, leaflets, laundry lists, candy wrappers. Hell, once I stopped at a graveyard just to read the tombstones. Newspaper today said unemployment passed the six million mark. That's near a quarter of the work force. Let you in on a little secret, Frank—he shifted his body closer to the table, and the stripes on his sleeves grew larger—I've been livin in this podunk town for two months. Only legal job I seen come up is bag boy at the Piggly Wiggly. In this life if you want reward—he tapped his forefinger against his temple—you gotta think in a different way.

Frank nodded his head in agreement, his body stiffening as the sheriff paused at their booth. With his swollen face and stout body, the sheriff resembled an ex-prizefighter, which, in fact, he was. In a fraternal gesture, Stokes offered his hand, and the sheriff clasped it. When the sheriff withdrew his hand, his fingers clutched an envelope, which he shifted to his trouser pocket.

For the Masons, Stokes said.

The sheriff gave a nod and proceeded to the door. Stokes jerked his coffee to his mouth and clattered the cup on the saucer. Frank looked at him with surprise. You a Mason?

Honorary member, Stokes said without a glimmer of a smile. Coincident with this remark, Billy rotated off his stool. He put on his hat, took a toothpick from the glass jar by the register and, waving to Rosa, left the diner without sparing Stokes or Frank a glance. What he had enjoyed observing most of all was Stokes's suave choreography with the sheriff.

THREE

Billy parked the car. As the engine ticked down in the heat, he observed the widow—Mrs. Grace O'Bannion—overseeing an ungainly moving operation on the sidewalk of the Congress Hotel. Two men in starched white uniforms were unloading an RCA radio from a Ford delivery van. Outlined by the streaming light behind her, Grace directed the movers with her raven black parasol.

Watch the side there. Don't scuff the bottom. *The Lone Ranger* rides tonight!

The first mover hummed *The William Tell Overture* while the second mover kept shouting: Hi-yo, Silver! Hi-yo, Silver!

Billy adjusted the silver fedora atop his silvery head, removed the toothpick from his mouth, combed his moustache and beard with his foldable comb, smoothed down the tails of his bolo tie, breathed in a whole breath and got out of the car. A hot breeze was wrapping Grace's mourning dress around her legs. The legacy of her youth—a ballerina in Denver, Rosa had said—was still evident in the muscular shaping of her calves. Each and every movement revealed her vitality and mocked the aura of death that surrounded her. How old could she be—forty-five, fifty? Entering inside the privileged orbit of her vision, Billy touched the brim of his hat with his forefinger.

Mrs. O'Bannion.

Dr. McCarty.

They told me at the desk a new resident was movin in, but they neglected to mention it was the town beauty.

On Grace's white oval face appeared two dimples. One was smaller than the other and it appeared and disappeared as if her cheek itself were winking. It was a face soft and lovely, shaded once by her wide-brimmed hat and once again by her parasol. Not for many years, Billy guessed, had any part of her face made acquaintance with the vulgar sun. He was about to ask her to call him by his first name when he got lost following the light in her blue eyes, and all other faculties, save sight, ceased to function.

Her smile darted from him as she turned to the movers—Careful, now! In the space of two seconds he had been blotted from her sight and extinguished from her mind. Billy's gaze clung to her retreating figure until she disappeared into the hotel entrance, and what remained of his composure drained from his belly to the soles of his feet. He had forgotten entirely why he had wanted to go to his room in the hotel. He was left with no memory, no will and no energy except what he could muster to ambulate his legs back to his car.

Ten minutes passed. Billy was now standing inside the sumptuous lobby of the Paramount Theater. Popcorn was popping before his very eyes in the automated popcorn machine that Al Jagu, the proprietor, had installed earlier that morning. Billy bought a bag of popcorn for a nickel and marveled that popcorn was now sold inside a movie palace instead of from a red wooden cart on the sidewalk.

In the middle of the first row Billy took his seat. He wanted to be as close to the screen as possible so he could enter inside the life of the central character. The lights dimmed, the curtains opened, a cartoon began and ended, and the curtains closed. Billy shifted in his seat. The picture was about to begin. He had seen the picture every day during its two-week engagement when it first opened two years ago. And now that the theater owner had brought it back for a one-week run, Billy had seen it every afternoon for the last six days.

The curtains opened again, this time over the MGM lion. The lion gave three cantankerous growls, and the title appeared on the screen: BILLY THE KID. Next came the actors' credits. The football star Johnny Mack Brown was playing the title role, and the silent film star Wallace Berry was playing Pat Garrett. At the end of the opening credits an official declaration appeared on the screen, a declaration that had required three earlier viewings for Billy to copy down correctly.

State of New Mexico
Office of the Governor
Santa Fe
September 25, 1930

It seems to me that this picture of Billy the Kid, though
it has taken liberties with the details of his life, pres-
ents a true drama of his career, and proves that this

gunfighter of early New Mexico played his part in the story of the West. Billy had a keen sense of justice that had been deeply outraged, and he set about with his gun and invincible courage to even up the scores, and along the way to restore to life on the range its personal liberty.

Yours very truly,

R.C. Dillon
Governor of New Mexico

As Billy read the familiar words, he could feel the energy of his youth surge through him. A keen sense of justice...invincible courage...Every young man in the West thought of himself as possessing those traits and, in his youth, Billy had been no exception. The plot of the movie Billy knew by heart. The plot concerned the Lincoln County war, a war that took place between powerful business interests and a group of small-time ranchers whom the Kid supported. In the movie the war lasted a few days, but in reality the war spanned a number of years, culminating in a spectacular five-day gun battle in which the Kid participated.

After one hundred minutes of wisecracks, gun play and general tomfoolery, the movie ended. The curtains closed, the lights came up and Billy let escape a sigh. At the end of each viewing he felt let down. In the movie the Kid had emerged victorious at the conclusion of the Lincoln County War. But the movie was missing an essential part of the real story. After the Lincoln County war was over, more than fifty men were arraigned, and yet all went free, except for the Kid, who was found guilty. The Kid was sentenced to hang by the neck until his body was dead, and hang he would have but for his audacious escape from the jail of the Lincoln County courthouse.

Thinking of the escape, Billy took out a notepad from his pocket and jotted down all the details he could think of, details he would later put in his book. And if some future historian wanted to dispute his account, let him try. For the last two years Billy had said to anyone who would listen that when his book was published, he would be the undisputed authority on the life of Billy the Kid, and the reason for this was that he was Billy the Kid himself.

$\sim$

At twilight, Billy directed his car toward the trailer camp. The sky took his breath away. The low sun had erected a flaming pillar from which exploded reds and oranges, pinks and whites, flooding the sky with a luminous beauty. He parked his car outside the trailer camp and strolled past the two privies that served over fifty house cars. Some of the house cars were makeshift, some do-it-yourselfers, others not house cars at all, but cars in their original state, towing genuine camping trailers. A few of these camping trailers had the entrance flaps pinned up, and inside you could see gasoline cook stoves and iceboxes and sets of drawers with no locks on them because everyone knew their contents weren't worth stealing. Now and again Billy stepped over a strand of the black spiderweb that conveyed electricity to all the dwellings. He was marveling at a Ford truck that some able farmer had carpentered into a two-story house car when from behind him came a man's voice: Help you, mister?

Billy wheeled around. Under a tarp that extended from a house car sat an elderly couple on a pair of folding chairs. They were drinking lemonades. Billy bade them good evening and asked where he might find Tommy. The wife tilted her tumbler to the right and told him to check the green auto tent. The husband asked if Billy was connected with the school, and Billy said no, he was just a friend.

Walking toward the green auto tent, Billy paused before a Model T that had been transformed into a white motor chapel, complete with steeple. Pondering the marvel, he imagined the man who must have built it. The man Billy conjured up in his mind had ignored for days the persistent whisperings in his head for fear he was going mad, until one night he listened to those whisperings for the first time and found they were not the profane ramblings he had feared, but a most sacred decree from on high—build a house of worship, said the whispering voice, build a house of worship on wheels—and the very next morning the man threw away his old life and bought lumber and paint, and with a cracked Bible crammed in his back pocket, carried out his solitary act of obedience. Billy thought any man who could thwart the expectations of the world and still survive the world was a man worthy of respect. He thought this even though he had never met a preacher he enjoyed listening to, save the one with the wooden arm who removed it during sermons to shake at his parishioners.

The green auto tent was nothing more than green canvas stretched over and around a Model T. As Billy neared the entrance, a man's voice reverberated within, a voice pitched to an angry B-sharp. If Tommy skipped school again, sounded the B-sharp, it wouldn't matter how old Tommy was, Tommy would get his backside tanned.

Bending down on his good knee, Billy propped Tommy's Wild West book by the side of the tent. As he rose, the tent billowed out—someone was leaning against the inside wall, and the tug in the fabric opened the front flap. A figure passed by the opening. It was Frank, the man from the diner.

FOUR

I t was a congenial enough atmosphere that night in the
dining room of the Congress Hotel. Long-term residents
outnumbered the traveling salesmen five to one, but most
of the salesmen were not considered strangers. Normally gregarious at the dinner hour, Billy had indicated a different temperament by bringing with him a sheaf of typed pages. At a small
table in the corner he proofread the pages, a correcting pencil
in his hand. Mulling over a sentence that described how to kill
a man with the least amount of effort, he looked up and met the
unblinking eyes of a bull elk whose triumphant antlers—eighty
pounds worth—sprang from the wall in fierce reproach. A trophy bull like this would have stood almost six feet at the withers
and at over twelve hundred pounds, hard to take down and keep
down, and at the very least you would need a .30 caliber bullet.
By comparison, killing a man didn't take much skill at all and
seemed less of a sin.

Earlier in the day someone had moved the radio from the Palm
Room into the dining room and now, to Billy's utter surprise, *Turkey in the Straw* was playing, a song from his youth.

Well, I had an old hen and she had a wooden leg,
Just the best old hen that ever laid an egg,
She laid more eggs than any hen on the farm,
But another little drink wouldn't do her any harm.

Went out to milk, and I didn't know how.
I milked the goat instead of the cow.
A monkey sittin on a pile of straw,
A-winkin at his mother-in-law.

The lyrics reminded him of the feeling he had when he was upside-down and wrong-side-out. And wasn't it how the Kid felt after each killing? There was a part of Billy that wanted to say yes, that's how it was, but the truth—the truth was dangerously different, and he knew it.

I came to the river and I couldn't get across.
So I paid five dollars for a big bay hoss.
Well, he wouldn't go ahead and he wouldn't stand still.
So he went up and down like an old saw mill.

The truth was that after the initial shock of killing someone, the body righted itself and a new feeling inhabited the shooter's body, a feeling of being indestructible. It was like wearing invisible body armor, like those Apache braves made bullet-proof by their medicine men, warriors who rode with their arms held high in front of a line of firing soldiers, with none of the bullets ever finding their mark. Yes, indestructible—that's how the Kid felt after killing a man. And powerful—the Kid felt powerful. Of this, Billy was certain. Pulling the trigger to kill a man released a bolt of energy that traveled through the shooter's body and traveled outside his body with the bullet itself. The way an arrow carried all the energy of the warrior in its tip. The way a tomahawk carried all the energy of the warrior in its blade. That same energy ricocheted back to the shooter the instant the bullet stole the life of another. As if the life force flowed back to the shooter across an invisible wire strung taut between vanquished and victor. As if the life force itself was absent of sin, had no moral quality and was merely a conveyance of pure power. Billy considered that in its original form the life force might have contained all the wisdom of the universe, but now the life force served the will of the Seen rather than the will of the Unseen, and Billy thought this alone could explain the desolation of the world.

The sound of heavy footsteps broke his reverie. Billy shifted in his chair and raised his hand in greeting. But to Dr. Benton, the dentist standing at the edge of the room, the raised hand was like the cursing gesture of an ancient race, and he rotated his beard around and followed its wispy point into the hallway.

Billy corrected ten more pages of his manuscript before heading up for the night. Halfway up the staircase, he snatched a rolled-up magazine from the air, tossed to him by the night clerk. Upstairs, he fit the iron key into the keyhole of his door and arched a look over his shoulder. From the other end of the hallway came the opening strains of *The William Tell Overture*. An orange light was pooling under the door as if an overflow of orchestral sound had splashed onto the floorboards. The music was replaced now with the commanding tones of the radio announcer: On a fiery horse with the speed of light, a cloud of dust and a hearty Hi-yo, Silver, The Lone Ranger rides again!

Some might say it was a providential twist of fate that landed Grace O'Bannion on Billy's floor, but Billy had known men who had entrusted their lives to Providence, and they had all died young, and even the locations of their burial plots were not particularly favored. Pushing open his door, Billy snapped on the overhead light and tossed his manuscript pages on the writing desk by the window. Off flew his hat to the hat rack, off flew the rubber band on the magazine, and flip-flip-flip went the pages until he found the notice of the auction he was looking for. He tore out the notice and taped it to the corner of his mirror.

WINCHESTER NEW MODEL 1873

Reputed to be the rifle of legend owned by Billy the Kid. Original sights, nice shootable bore, a few light pits. Original wood excellent with carbine style buttplate and no handling marks. Metal is a plum brown patina with good blue color in the protected areas. Markings are excellent, action crisp, complete with dust cover and saddle ring.

On taking his seat at his writing desk, Billy reached over a raft of titles for a book he had borrowed from the library, *The Authentic Life of Billy the Kid*. A copper bookmark in the shape of a rifle indicated where he had left off the day before. From a drawer he pulled out a fresh sheet of paper and sharpened his pencil. Note-taking always gave him a feeling of great accomplishment, despite the minimal effort required. The feeling was different when he was writing his book. He had discovered that writing prose was not unlike writing a song—what you needed, above all, was a good melody. Sometimes in the thrilling excitement of composition he thought he had found his melody, and later he would read over what he had written, and the melody would be gone. When the melody did come, not fleetingly, but enduringly, there would be firings around the edges of his scalp like flashes of gunpowder, and he knew then he could keep what he had written. Still, he did not consider himself a writer, never wanted to be a writer, didn't know any writers except the editor of the newspaper, and the editor didn't write so much as worthily opine. Billy's talents lay in other fields—dentistry and guitar being two of them. But there was a story in him that wanted letting out, a story longer than he could tell in a song, so he had no choice but to unburden himself in prose.

By the time Billy had turned off his desk lamp, light was pouring through his blinds from a full strawberry moon. Outside his window he could hear the growling engine of a motorcar. He stood up from his desk and peered through a corner of the blinds. Two men were getting out of a car across the street. Both were formally attired. Holding onto each other's arms for support, they advanced toward a red-brick building, the glowing tips of their cigarettes wobbling in the dark, and when they reached an unpainted door, the one whose hand was the steadiest rapped out a code.

A slat flew open, uncovering a Judas hole. A conversation took place on either side of the door, the sounds overlapping each other, and Billy couldn't make out a single word. Abruptly the door swung open, revealing a big-limbed doorman with a fleshy face who was breathing through his mouth. He retreated a step, and Stokes emerged into the half-light, clutching his black lapels. He said good evening to the two men and ushered them inside with a low wave, and the door thudded shut.

Lying in his bed that night, Billy listened to the sounds rising from the street. In an interval of silence he could make out a faint shuffling. By now, Billy knew what the sound meant. It was the sound of desperate men on the move in shoes that swamped their feet. It was the sound of desperate men scouring the streets for baskets of food. It was the sound of men fighting against futility and despair in a desperate attempt to remember who they once were and what they once wanted to become.

As the shuffling faded away, there was the sharp report of a car door slamming. Two boisterous voices followed. The voices were arguing about what kind of alcohol makes a man the most violent. Billy's thoughts returned to Frank and his association with Stokes. Killing and getting killed were part of the bootlegging business. If Frank got himself killed, what would happen to Tommy? Billy's fretting about Frank robbed him of half a night's sleep, and when the wheel of sleep finally turned, it turned fitfully, and when Billy woke up the next morning it was with a premonition that all would end badly.

FIVE

——————

By chance Billy saw Frank the next morning—hottest weather in five years, bragged *The Pueblo Chieftain*. On the way to the drugstore in his car, under a blue sky unrelieved by a single white cloud, Billy passed a mechanic's garage, and there, profiled in the window, was Frank, and on Frank's face was a look of astonishment.

Billy could guess the reason why. A week earlier, at the same garage, Billy had stopped by with a flat tire, and through the window he had seen three mechanics, slick with sweat, disassembling a Model A. Two of the mechanics he had known for years, and they invited him to be an onlooker to their ingenuity. As their hands flew over the car, the spare tire spawned ten warm bottles of Mexican hooch, the seats twenty a piece, the steering column a half dozen and the chassis a dozen. Everywhere the car gave birth to another gleaming litter.

Billy left Frank to his fate in the garage and traveled through half a mile of hazy heat before arriving at the drugstore. Inside the drugstore the ceiling fan was pushing around a brick of stale air in a child's game that accomplished nothing. Billy bought a tube of toothpaste—the first time he had ever bought toothpaste from a druggist instead of a salesman. Feeling very modern, he left the store and crossed a hot yard of sidewalk to his car. Reaching for the ignition key in his pocket, he heard the pounding of feet and the cry of the grocer—Thief!

The flying shape almost knocked Billy to the pavement. Clutching at the air, he caught Tommy's wrist. As Tommy broke loose, a Mars chocolate bar fell from his hand, followed by an apple that gave a joyful bounce before rolling to a stop against Billy's boot.

A moment later the grocer was standing before Billy, his chest heaving, his brow spangled with sweat. His flushed corpulence lightened a shade as Billy took out his change purse. Billy explained he was friends with the boy, and the grocer said Billy should keep better company then, the boy was obviously working for a gangster, he could always spot a gangster's apprentice, he knew for a fact that gangsters were recruiting children as young as five. Billy listened to the canard with a solemn face and counted out each of the eight cents that was owing.

As this transaction of high finance was concluding, a Stutz Saloon automobile glided to a stop before the drugstore. The engine was murmuring deferential sounds as the back door lifted out, disclosing an unlit cigar and the sleek body of Stokes. As Stokes proceeded to the drugstore, he gave his arm a jerk, which precipitated a pistol into his hand. The reedy young chauffeur, in the still-murmuring Stutz, did not look up. Under his peaked cap he was studying the funnies section of the newspaper. A soundless laugh convulsed his face, and Billy could see he had buck teeth and a large overbite. Meantime, the grocer, never faltering in his detective work, strode off to search for young gangsters climbing the monkey bars in the park—or so Billy presumed.

Coast is clear, Billy said in a soft voice.

Tommy rose from behind a nearby car, ranged his eyes over the street and bounded over. Billy slapped the Mars bar in the boy's hand and handed him the apple.

Don't be stealin, son.

Billy the Kid stole lots of stuff.

Billy the Kid? What do you know about Billy the Kid?

Tommy took out his Wild West book, said thanks—that was for Billy returning it—and read from inside the front cover: In his career as an outlaw, Billy the Kid robbed banks and stagecoaches, burglarized stores and waylaid travelers.

Waylaid travelers, Billy said, shaking his head back and forth. That's the trouble with books. They never tell you the truth. The Kid was friendly to travelers, he didn't waylay em. And he never robbed a bank or a stagecoach in his life. And he never held up a store neither. That book has got the Kid mixed up with Jesse James.

How do you know?

You'd be surprised what I know, Tommy.

Like what?

Like we're goin to have a duster later today.

How do you know?

Read the sky.

Read what?

The sky, Billy said. And here's somethin else I know. Any moment now that man will break into a run. He motioned with his head to a man across the street, garbed in a uniform of juniper green.

How do you know that? Tommy said.

Cause he'd be the truant officer, Billy said.

A look of alarm flashed in Tommy's face. Before Billy could say another word, Tommy was a blur of legs, and the truant officer, in fast pursuit, was breaking several ordinances of common decency—befouling the sidewalk with his spit, profaning the air with his language, and making a public nuisance of himself by smacking the hoods of braking cars as he cut across the street.

The pistol shots, when they came, were three in number.

Stokes burst from the drugstore in gladiator strides, flexing his smooth hands that had no gun in them now, and raising his eyes to the glaring sun as if to acknowledge his only rival. His glance lowered and fell on his car. The chauffeur was on his feet, holding the rear door open. He had an expression of sleepy unconcern, as if to say he would rather be lying on a couch like Dagwood with a newspaper over his face than standing upright and working for a living. Stokes paused before the open door, popped a match on his thumbnail, lit his cigar between his fingers, snapped the match to the gutter and took a leisurely puff. Throwing away the cigar the next moment, he climbed inside the car, and by the time he had opened the liquor compartment to reach for a drink, the Stutz was ferrying him away.

When Billy rushed inside the drugstore, he almost stumbled over the body that was sprawled across the floor. The dead man wore a pink suit and was lying supine in a widening circle of blood. No bullet wound was visible. He had been shot in the side or the back, and the force of the impact had spun him around before he collapsed.

The eyes of the crouching druggist were level with the prescription counter, and Billy found himself ludicrously addressing the top of a bald head.

Pete, you call the sheriff?

As if on cue, the sheriff materialized from behind an aisle of dry goods. And now the female soda jerk rose from behind the soda counter, and two trembling customers got up from the floor, and the assistant druggist peered around another aisle. The sheriff bent down to check the victim for a pulse, glanced up at the druggist and told him to call the undertaker. Billy regarded the sheriff intently and asked who the victim was. The sheriff hurried to the door, saying the man was nobody, a small-timer from Phoenix, everyone called him Delivery, nobody knew his real name.

Billy called out: So what you fixin to do?

Do? The sheriff stopped at the door and looked at him incredulously. He'll be buried in a grave without a marker. His virtues will be remembered by his fellow men, his sins by his maker.

No, what you fixin to do about the killin?

No one cares about a dead bootlegger, the sheriff said and banged through the door.

SIX

The lunch crowd that day filled Earl's Diner to capacity. At Billy's booth Rosa was rolling an ice cube over her face and telling him the special today was lousy. Billy changed his order to a grilled cheese sandwich with a side of applesauce and a slice of Rocky Ford melon. Pouring out a glass of ice water, Rosa spoke to him in a whisper: Is it true Sheriff Jack Warden was in the drugstore during the shootin this morning and did nothin?

Billy was pensive for a moment. Rosa, this is still the West.

Rosa looked at him expressively, and Billy raised the sweating glass to his mouth. Rosa was about to launch into an argument when the bell above the door tinkled. Grace, garbed in her widow's weeds, was casting her eyes about for a table.

When you goin to speak to her? Rosa said.

Why, just yesterday I tipped my hat to her and said hello.

Well, ain't you just Mr. Slap-Happy and How-de-do.

Rosa, she's in mourning.

After three years, it ain't mourning, it's moaning. Sides, you're neighbors now, ain't you?

Stepping away, she gave him half a smile that communicated everything else she wanted to say. Billy saw the two women talking, and twice Rosa inclined her head in his direction. Next thing he knew, Grace was settling into his booth, and the muscle of his heart was working twice as hard as it had been one minute before.

Grace removed her mourning hat and gloves. Her hands were even whiter than her face. She glanced up at Billy with her blue eyes blinking, and Billy felt a stitch of unjustifiable joy.

Thank you for your kindness, Dr. McCarty. I have to eat when I'm hungry, or I get cranky. Tuna salad, please, Rosa. Separate checks.

Rosa gave Billy a wink before whirling away. Billy was still schooling his heart to a slower rhythm when Grace leaned toward him, her blue eyes seeking his, and his heart took off again. She opened her mouth and spoke again with her low musical voice, but on this occasion no tranced words floated out to enwrap him in a perfumed mystery. Her voice, when it reached his ears, was serrated with a quiet anger.

Dr. McCarty, one thing I've often wondered. Did you know my husband at all?

Her red lips parted. Her white teeth were perfectly aligned, and Billy surmised she had never worn braces—platinum, gold or silver. Before he could answer her question, she said her husband would never have let a murder in a drugstore go unanswered.

Your husband was a very brave man, Mrs. O'Bannion. He died for what he believed in.

Grace dabbed her napkin at a faint wet line above her lip. He died, Dr. McCarty, because three years ago some no-account bootlegger shot him in the gut. You didn't know my husband, very well, did you?

No, ma'am, I didn't. See, he went to Dr. Benton for his dental.

And he wasn't a Mason.

No, ma'am.

And you are.

Yes, ma'am.

And Masons don't admit Catholics into their organization.

See, personally, I'm not in agreement with that.

Not good enough for the Masons, yet good enough to die for the privilege of protecting this town.

Rosa interrupted with their orders, and as Grace thanked her, a radiance suffused her cheeks, and Billy was confounded by the return of his giddiness. Billy glanced up. Rosa was lingering beside the table.

Want to join us, Rosa?

I'm waitin for you to try the applesauce.

You make it yourself?

It's Mott's.

Who's Mott?

Mott's is the name of the company that owns the factory.

They make applesauce in a factory now?

My kids love it.

Bet you serve it up for dessert, Billy said, spooning up a mouthful.

So what you think?

Billy swallowed and made a face.

It appears Dr. McCarty is a traditionalist, Grace said.

Billy shook his head to the contrary. It's just that canned applesauce has no romance, he said.

Romantic applesauce, Grace said. What an imagination.

You should hear what he says about the Rocky Ford melon, Rosa said, placing her fingertips on Billy's shoulder. It's enough to make a girl blush. Oh, you need more water.

She returned to the counter for the pitcher, and Grace leaned forward in her seat. What is it about you, Dr. McCarty? When did you decide to reinvent yourself?

Billy took a bite of the Rocky Ford melon and asked what she meant.

I understand you're writin a book about your life.

Yes, he was.

You really think people are goin to believe you're Billy the Kid?

Yes, he did.

Well, to begin with, Billy the Kid died some fifty years ago, she said.

He pointed out the obvious error.

Dr. McCarty, you're a dentist.

He corrected her.

A retired dentist, then. And you want people to think you were once a famous outlaw? Forgive me for sayin so, Dr. McCarty, but don't you think it's just a tad preposterous?

Rosa arrived with the ice water and freshened their glasses. Billy gripped her forearm before she could leave. Rosa, tell Mrs. O'Bannion here who I really am.

Is this one of em trick questions?

Just tell her.

Rosa placed her forefinger on her cheek as she composed her thoughts aloud. Well, let's see. He's Dr. McCarty who came to town eighteen years ago and fixed my teeth—she grinned a gargoyle grin to show her straightened teeth—after I left Dr. Benton, that is. Oh, and he's also Billy the Kid.

Billy smiled in triumph as Rosa swung the pitcher away. Grace lowered her fork to her plate. And what would you have done, Mr. Billy the Kid, if my husband had arrested you for all the killin you did?

Called up the newspapers.

The newspapers?

Sure. Thataway my story would be heard.

And just what is your story?

That your past don't determine your future.

You're wrong there, Dr. McCarty. The past is your future.

Billy took a sip of water and lowered his glass. Mrs. O'Bannion, if the future is just an extension of the past, you'd be the same person you were ten years ago.

I am the same person I was ten years ago, exceptin some minor physical details.

Are you the same person you were thirty years ago?

In the most important respects, I believe I am.

Mrs. O'Bannion, I don't think you're the same person you were a month ago, or a week ago. You're not even the same person you were a few minutes ago.

Grace let her fork clink against her plate. Her color deepened. The difference between the person who entered the diner and the person sittin at this booth is this small, she said, her thumb touching her forefinger. And that's only because I'm perturbed now.

Billy made the identical gesture with his thumb and forefinger. A bullet, Mrs. O'Bannion, could travel through that amount of difference and kill a man.

And you would know about that, bein as you are Billy the Kid.

And I would know about that, bein as I am Billy the Kid.

Grace lowered her head and took several earnest bites of her salad. When Rosa brought over the checks, Billy felt a measure of relief, but the awkwardness of the meal resumed the moment Rosa left the table.

Separately, Billy and Grace paid their checks, but they walked to the door together. Billy held it open, and it was his graciousness that made Grace's dimples reappear.

Watch it there, Billy said over his shoulder.

Stokes had brushed by Grace, jostling her against the doorjamb. Making a slight bow, Stokes asked for forgiveness in a pastel tone suitable for respectable women and the infirm. With a flutter of her eyelids Grace acknowledged his apology and was out the door, becoming incandescent in the shimmering afternoon. Stokes had not moved from the doorway, and Billy took a hard look at his face. The cut corners of the man's mouth were like the tips of bowie knives. Stokes crooked his neck at an angle and looked at Billy with searching eyes.

Who the hell are you?

Billy.

What's your last name?

The Kid.

Stokes's face broke into a wide grin of pleasure that displayed the even front teeth of his dental plate.

Well, I'll say this, Mr. Billy the Kid, you got guts. They're in short supply in this town. Having delivered himself of this pronouncement, he withdrew his gaze, turned his striped back and strode inside.

Pacing outside on the sidewalk was a young man with dark features, wearing a torn denim jacket. As Billy emerged from the diner, the young man rushed over. El Chivato, he said.

Opening his swollen jaw, the young man pointed to an upper molar. Billy peered at the tooth.

It's gone, Gabriel. The tooth has gone. Better see Dr. Benton.

No, Billy. *No me gusta Dr. Benton.*

Billy raised his arms in a helpless gesture. *No te puedo ayudar.*

I let you ride my horse, Gabriel said.

You bought a horse?

Si, en Texas.

You bought a horse in Texas?

A Mustang Paint, fourteen hands high. You ride her, shoot two silver dollars in the air. Blam! Blam! Like old days, no?

Billy waggled his gammy left leg for Gabriel's benefit. Look at me, Gabriel. The old days are over. Last month I retired, sold my instruments and my chair.

Gabriel was on the verge of protesting when Dr. Benton strutted toward them, leading with a tuft of his gnomish beard. Billy hailed him, and Dr. Benton halted in mid-stride, twirled around like a marionette and strutted off in the direction whence he came. Gabriel trotted after him, shouting for him to stop, but Dr. Benton held his headlong course. Billy shook his head at the wonderment of it all and turned toward his car.

From ten yards behind came a shrill voice: Billy the Kid, I got a little present for you!

Recognizing the voice, Billy glanced over his shoulder at a young boy of five dressed as a cowboy. What you got for me, Pat?

A twenty-five-cent piece I plugged at twenty yards!

And I've got a little present for you, Pat. A nickel I plugged at thirty yards!

Darn it, Billy the Kid, now I got to go out and ruin a nice shiny ten-cent piece!

Billy laughed. The routine came from the Billy the Kid movie the young cowboy had seen three times. The mother of the boy had indulged her son in his cowboy fantasies ever since he had contracted polio two years ago. Billy saluted the young cowboy and opened the car door, but before he could lift a leg inside, the young cowboy drew a gun from his holster and limped a step toward him. Gunslinger, he said with as much menace as he could wring out of his shrill treble. Without a moment's hesitation Billy fired an imaginary pistol over his shoulder, and the young cowboy jerked backwards and collapsed in mortal agony against his mother's skirts. Billy climbed into his car, hit the electric starter button with his boot heel, gave the car some gas and took off.

The car had gone less than a block when Billy turned the wheel sharply to the curb. Reaching into the back seat, he pulled up Tommy by the collar.

Don't hurt me or nothin, Tommy said, his body trembling.

What are you doin back there, Tommy?

I just, I just, I just.

You just what?

I just heard about the killin in the drugstore, and I saw the man in the striped suit walkin in my direction, and I got scared and wanted to hide.

Why were you scared?

Well, he's a bad man, ain't he?

Well, he's not a good man. Listen, there's still a few hours of school left. How about I drop you off?

It's lunch time right now. I got another half hour of nothin to do.

Billy's eyes shifted to Tommy's hair, which was plastered to his skull in one large greasy lump. In that case we got time to get you some soap and shampoo, he said.

I can't take nothin from a stranger.

Well, I'm not givin, Billy said.

Well, I don't rightly understand what you're sayin then.

Billy took the car into the street again. I'll show you what exactly I'm sayin.

They traveled without exchanging a word until Billy reached the outskirts of town. Pulling over to the gravel shoulder, he climbed out of the car, opened the trunk and took out a canvas bag. After walking a few paces in the chaparral, he knelt down beside a spikey green plant and examined its leaves and flower. From the canvas bag Billy produced a four-pronged digging fork, a rag and a Belknap bench hatchet. Glancing up, he called over to Tommy who was staring at him through the lowered passenger window. Come here and watch what I do.

Tommy got out of the car, trotted over and plunked himself down.

First, we thank the spirit of the Yucca plant on account we're goin to take its life, Billy said.

Tommy made a face. There's no spirit of the Yucca plant, he said.

The Mescalero Apaches tell it different.

Billy leaned toward the plant and spoke softly to it in the Mescalero dialect. And when he had finished, Tommy looked at him with eyes wide and round.

Where'd you learn to speak like that?

When I was a young man, a few years older than you are now, I had the need to leave civilization for a spell. I joined a band of

Mescalero Apaches who had left the reservation and made friends with an old Mescalero.

Tommy was silent for a moment. Geronimo was an Apache, right?

Yes, he was, Tommy. He was a leader of the Chiricahua Apaches. They say he had the power of the coyote.

Power of the coyote?

He knew how to become invisible and that's why no one could ever catch him.

But they captured him. So what happened to his power?

Geronimo was never captured, Tommy. He surrendered. And only because his people were starvin.

So what's your power?

I'm fast with a gun, Billy said.

How'd you get so fast?

The old Mescalero, he told me that when I was a young man sleepin in the desert one night, the pronghorn became my teacher in my sleep and that's how I got so fast.

You believe that?

I don't know if I believe it or not, but I don't have a better explanation. See how I dig up the whole plant? Now watch how I wipe down the roots with this rag and get rid of all the loose earth. You have a pocketknife?

No, sir.

A pocketknife is among the most useful tools ever created. Now watch carefully.

Using his pocketknife, Billy peeled off the outer skin of a root, leaving the hard white flesh exposed. Handing his pocketknife to Tommy, he told him to do the same to all the roots. Tommy peeled each root down to the white flesh, and when he was finished, Billy said he had done a fine job.

Picking up the hatchet, Billy slapped the handle in Tommy's hand. Now chop the roots into pieces as big as your fist, he said. You'll get about a dozen large pieces.

When Tommy had finished with the chopping, Billy told him to chop up three of the largest pieces into smaller pieces the size of hailstones, and Tommy did so. Next, Billy drew from his canvas bag a piece of cloth and a large stone that fit into Tommy's hand and told Tommy to mush up the hailstone pieces on the cloth. Once Tommy had completed the task, Billy spread out the mushed-up pieces beside the larger pieces. He said all the pieces would dry in the sun, and he would collect them at sunset. There would be plenty of pieces of shampoo, he said, along with some thick bars of soap. Tommy said all this bathing and hair washing was something he would rather avoid, and Billy said it was part of a gunslinger's job to look good, and with these words Tommy's eyes opened wider, and on the ride to the school, Tommy asked Billy about his time living with the Mescalero Apaches, and Billy answered every question with such knowledge and certainty that Tommy believed he was telling the truth.

Arriving at the school, Billy told Tommy not to ditch school any more, and Tommy promised he wouldn't, and Billy said a promise was a serious thing, and Tommy said he knew what a promise meant and jumped out of the car. Billy watched to make sure he entered the building, and settling back in the driver's seat, kept his gaze fixed on the entrance in case Tommy made a break for it. But after a few minutes Billy's eyes closed shut. When he awoke, he glanced at his pocket watch. He was late for the Spit 'n' Argue.

SEVEN

—

Beneath the genteel shade of the Thatcher building there ran a brass railing, three feet off the ground, that had served as the headquarters for the Spit 'n' Argue Club for forty years. Two of the members were now occupying that railing, and since two members constituted a quorum, the meeting had begun. As usual, the meeting had no set agenda, but was a free-for-all discussion with no recording secretary present, for the discussion consisted of broken shards of speech that could only be pieced together by a linguist specializing in the cuneiform of an ancient language.

As important as the arguing was the spitting. Since the day of the club's inauguration the members had stained the trunk of a shade tree with long streams of amber juice, the trunk taking on the sepia color of an old photograph, the members themselves sepia-skinned and looking like the ancient progenitors of a sacred and immemorial tradition. One member was a gun dealer, the other a retired bricklayer. Together they had spent so many years spitting and arguing that they had mimicked each other's facial expressions until people who didn't know any better thought they were brothers, or possibly twins.

As Billy came toward the brass railing, the bricklayer gave him a welcoming nod and let loose a stream of juice that splattered an anthill at the base of the tree.

Dust storm a-comin, the gun dealer said, lifting his face to the brooding sky.

Billy took up his perch between the two men. From his left rear pocket he drew out a new package of Days-o-Life. In the old days he had bought his plug in the general store and kept it wrapped in an oilskin, but now you could buy a plug in the drugstore, and it came wrapped in a cellophane wrapper. Using his pocketknife, Billy cut a circle around the cellophane. If he was not careful, he might tear the cellophane down the length of the plug, and air would wick out the moisture, and dry tobacco would pebble into his pocket. Easing the tip of the plug out of the cellophane, he bit it off. He pushed the plug to the side of his cheek, and his mouth began weeping. Out of habit he licked his forefinger and held it up in the air, but the breeze had died. Notching back his head he let out his first spit of the day and leaned back.

A shard flew from the gun dealer: Billy lunchin with the widow today.

A shard flew from the bricklayer: Billy goin soft.

The gun dealer spoke with a wounded voice: True, Billy goin soft?

In the branches above, a yellowthroat wearing a bandit's mask was chanting *which-is-it? which-is-it? which-is-it?* Billy darkened the trunk of the tree with more juice. To the men and the yellowthroat: Why, I reckon I've been goin soft for years.

Verily, the bricklayer said.

Verily, the gun dealer said.

A gust of wind stirred the leaves overhead, and there came a downpour of fine dust. The gun dealer sneezed like buckshot, wiped his nose with a rag and asked about the shootout in the drugstore. True, Billy, you almost tripped over the body?

The bricklayer jumped in: Think, Billy, you could've taken Stokes in younger days?

Billy opened his mouth to reply, but the gun dealer flung out a response before Billy could answer: Course, Billy, when younger, could've taken Stokes.

Listening to his friends argue about his storied past, Billy's mind capered at the edge of a humorous abyss. He pushed the plug deeper into his cheek. I believe I could've taken Stokes as a young man, Billy said. In fact, I'm sure of it.

Verily, the bricklayer said.

Verily, the gun dealer said.

The bricklayer reached over and grabbed Billy's arm. Tell again about your first kill, Billy. Tell, tell.

Billy waved the request aside.

Come on, the gun dealer said, grabbing Billy's other arm. Tell about Windy Cahill. Tell true, Billy, tell true.

Billy hesitated for a moment to judge the level of interest of his friends. Their eyes were wide with anticipation, and their bodies were tilting toward him. Billy took a breath and eased into the story.

Two hundred and fifty pounds, Billy said. That's how much Windy weighed.

Newspaper reported a small man, the gun dealer said.

Well, the newspapers were wrong. He was a big man. I remember his nose was broken and one of his front teeth was discolored.

Dentist in you even then, the bricklayer said.

No doubt, Billy said.

Windy a blacksmith, the gun dealer said, bringing Billy back on topic.

That he was, Billy said. He forged horseshoes, axes, pots, nails, anything you can think of for the Camp Grant Army Post in Arizona.

Shackles? the bricklayer said.

He did forge shackles, Billy said. And a month before our big fight he had shackled my wrists and ankles when he caught me stealin government saddles.

Was you stealin em, Billy? the gun dealer said. Tell true, Billy, tell true.

Billy lowered his head and smiled. Naturally, I was stealin em. An outlaw has to make a livin. I was Billy the Kid back then.

Verily, the bricklayer said.

Verily, the gun dealer said.

Tell what happened, night of August 17, 1877, the bricklayer said with barely suppressed excitement.

August 17th was the night that changed my life forever, Billy said. I'm in the middle of a hand of poker, and from across the room there's Windy Cahill calling me a no-account thief and a baseless liar.

Called you a liar? Like you made up stuff? The bricklayer inclined his head toward the gun dealer, and the gun dealer opened his eyes in mock surprise. Billy picked up on the exchange but continued his story nevertheless.

He did call me a liar at that.

So what'd ye do? the gun dealer said.

I set my cards on the table. I strike a match, and I hold up a cigarette of fine-cut tobacco. I look up at Windy and I say: *Con su licencia, señor.*

What that mean? the gun dealer said.

It was a gesture of politeness, Billy said. I picked it up when I was livin among the Mexicans. I can't say Windy understood what I was sayin because next thing I know he pushes himself from the bar and leadin with his beer, takes three steps forward and says I'm nothin but a pimp.

What'd ye do then? the bricklayer said.

Tell true, Billy, tell true, the gun dealer said.

Well, I turn to the dealer, and I ask for two more cards. And only after I've reorganized my hand do I mutter under my breath the name Windy Cahill, slippin in a certain choice epithet at the end. Well, that Windy—he crosses the last few yards to the poker table and asks me to repeat what I said. I say there's no point in repeatin it, it's common knowledge.

Made Windy mad, the bricklayer said.

Hornet mad, the gun dealer said.

So mad, Billy said, he throws his beer in my face and demands to know what I said. This time I fold my cards on the table. I wipe the beer off my face with my sleeve, pick up my cards again, fan em out and say in a voice loud enough to be heard by everyone that Windy Cahill is—

A son of a bitch! the bricklayer said.

Let Billy tell, the gun dealer said. He don't need your help!

Son of a bitch is just what I call him, Billy said. And that gets him madder than ever.

What'd he do? the gun dealer said. Kick your chair out?

Thought Billy goin to tell the story, the bricklayer said.

He does kick my chair out, Billy said, and sends me flyin to the floor. And before I have time to react, he hurls his empty beer glass at my face, catchin me right here. You can still make out the scar, see?

Billy pointed to a small scar on his cheek, beneath his beard, and the spitters leaned in for a closer look. Of course you can't see it much anymore, Billy said, drawing back. But, anyway, Windy jumps on top of me, and we go thrashin and bangin about the floor. But I weigh next to nothin and I'm no match for his heft, and next thing I know, he's pinnin my arms to the floor with his knees, and I'm thinkin I'm a goner. Billy shook his head at the memory.

Go on, go on, the brick layer said, angling his head toward him.

Tell true, Billy, tell true, the gun dealer said, shifting closer on the brass railing.

Billy hesitated a moment to collect his thoughts and continued. Windy's throwin punch after punch to my face, but somehow—I don't know how I did it—I manage to wriggle out my arm and slide out my pistol from my waistband, and then it happens.

What happens? the gun dealer said.

The roar from the pistol, Billy said, glancing from one man to the other.

The roar from the pistol, both spitters said in unison.

If someone had entered the cantina at just that moment, Billy said, they would have seen twenty-three patrons frozen on the spot. As if the roar from the pistol had caused all their joints to seize up. As if some deer-clad Apache medicine man had whirred his Izze-kloth medicine cord above his head and stolen all power of motion from the room.

Stolen all the power of motion, the gun dealer said.

From the room, the bricklayer said.

Now, outside the saloon there's a horse, Billy said. It belongs to my friend John Murphey. And John's horse whinnies, breakin the spell in the cantina, and people move about again. But before any of em could draw a gun, I gain my feet, gain the door and gain the street. I'd shot Windy in the gut, and now I was a gunslinger. I became a killer two days later when Windy died.

A silence fell over the men as they absorbed the gravity of the pronouncement. It was as if they had heard the story for the very first time.

How'd ye get out of town? the bricklayer said.

I borrow John Murphey's horse, Billy said, and I trade it for one horse after another on the way to New Mexico. And three weeks later I pay a friend of mine to bring back John Murphey's horse, and he gives John some money for the inconvenience. So that's the story, gentlemen, of the first time I killed a man, as told to you by Billy the Kid himself.

Verily, the gun dealer said.

Verily, the bricklayer said.

Across the street a tow-headed boy was walking with his head down. Billy squinted under his hat. It was Tommy. A pair of gap-toothed twins, wearing identical scowls, appeared to be teasing him, and Billy heard one of the boys calling Tommy a dunce cap. Tommy raised his head, clenching his fists as if spoiling for a fight, and at that moment Billy gave a whistle, and when Tommy whirled around and caught sight of him, he changed his course and walked swiftly over. With solemn formality Billy introduced Tommy to the Spit 'n' Argue Club. Duly impressed but apprehensive, Tommy shifted his schoolbooks from one arm to another.

What you want to be, son, when you grow up? the gun dealer said.

Bricklayer? the bricklayer said.

Your own gun and ammo shop? the gun dealer said.

Or outlaw it like your friend here, the bricklayer said, gesturing to Billy.

Billy waved his hand to change the topic, and this caused the bricklayer to slap his knee with enthusiasm. He not told you, Tommy? the bricklayer said. This man here be Billy the Kid.

Tommy's eyes had flown from one man to another, and now they flashed with annoyance.

You think we joshin you? the gun dealer said, his eyes twinkling.

From Tommy's expression it was clear he wasn't in a mood to be tested. His voice leaped two octaves. Everyone knows Billy the Kid died when he was twenty-one. Shot in the back by Pat Garrett!

The words had the effect of propelling Billy to his feet. He clapped a hand on Tommy's shoulder and said he would buy him an ice cream float. He raised his eyes to the sky. There was still an hour or so before the dust storm. He had not gone ten yards with Tommy before the gun dealer cupped his hands to his mouth.

Tell true, Billy, tell true!

Now the bricklayer cupped his hands to his mouth: Don't hold nothin back, Kid!

The men hooted and barked with delight. Billy looked over his shoulder and gave them both a look. The look was admonishing and humorous and which side Billy was leaning more toward was impossible to tell.

EIGHT

———

The cast-iron stools of the drugstore had cherry vinyl seats with the scalloped edges of a bottle cap. Billy and Tommy rested their elbows on the counter and watched the female soda jerk prepare Tommy's order. First, she pumped a river of dark syrup into the soda water, covering two scoops of vanilla ice cream that were whispering secrets to each other in bubbles. Next, she added three drops of phosphoric acid. That was to cut the sweetness. In a finishing touch she dipped a spoon into a large glass container and dolloped out two scoops of whipped cream.

Billy started on a chocolate malt. With the first pull on his straw he was back in New York City, he was a young boy and he was stealing a slab of chocolate from the grocer's and he was sprinting down the street with the cries of the grocer in his ear and he was eating and running and running and laughing until he had whittled down the chocolate to the size of a silver dollar and he wouldn't eat this last piece, no, not ever, but the grocer's cries had died upon his ears and the chocolate had softened in his palm and he opened his hand and skimmed his teeth over the dark sweetness and all eating and running and running and laughing came to an end.

Billy waited until Tommy clinked his spoon against the bottom of his fountain glass before speaking. Those boys who were teasin you back there. What was that all about, son?

Nothin.

Heard one of em call you a dunce cap.

It don't matter to me.

Well, it matters to me because you're my friend now. If they give you any more trouble, any trouble at all, you come and tell me, y'hear?

Are you really Billy the Kid?

Billy called over to the soda jerk: Who am I, Lucinda?

Lucinda, a recent high school graduate, was wiping the counter. She turned and gave an answer that was flavored with a smile. Why, unless I'm mistaken, you're none other than Billy the Kid.

So you're Billy the Kid? Tommy said. Even though you're supposed to be dead?

See, Tommy, Pat Garrett and I were long-time friends. I'd romanced the sister of Pat's second wife, and long before Pat was ever sheriff we had worked together as self-reliant cattlemen, you might say. Pat was a respectable Southern gentleman, raised on a plantation in Louisiana, had a white linen suit, droopin moustache, all of that stuff. Had a lot of different careers, on both sides of the law. So what happens is Pat kills this other bandit, tells everyone it's me, and we split the reward money for my death.

Did the other bandit look like you? Tommy said.

No, he was taller and had a chipped front tooth, but he was young like me, and no one knew what I looked like so it didn't matter. Billy paused and added: See, truth is a strange thing, Tommy.

There's the truth and there's what people believe is the truth, and sometimes what they believe is stronger than the real truth and sometimes it's even truer than the real truth.

Did you really kill twenty-five men?

Ten.

Only ten?

Ten not enough for you?

What was it like, all that killin, killin, always killin?

Billy slapped a coin on the counter and said it was time to go. Tommy accompanied Billy to his car and asked if Billy still had his guns. Billy braced his foot against the car's running board. What do you know about my guns?

Colt Double-Action Thunderers. Still have em?

Billy's eyes opened a little. I have em.

What about your Lightnings?

No.

Colt Single-Action Army?

No. Sorry to disappoint you, Tommy.

Is it true you once shot a man just for snorin?

Billy laughed at the old rumor. No, that was John Wesley Hardin, the Texas desperado.

Is it true you were you the most wanted man in America?

I was the most wanted man in the Southwest.

Billy read the disappointment in Tommy's face.

I just didn't kill enough men, Tommy. Guess you could say I lacked ambition.

I read about how you gunned down an unarmed man, Tommy said. His name was Texas Red Grant, he was your second kill, and you killed him at a bar near Fort Sumner.

Texas Red wasn't unarmed.

Well, that's what I read.

Let me tell you a little bit about Texas Red, Billy said, shifting his foot on the running board and resting his elbow on his knee. See, Texas Red had been boastin for weeks he would kill Billy the Kid if he ever ran across him. He said Billy the Kid pushed everyone around, and Texas Red wasn't the type to take it on the chin the way most people did. So this one night he was makin his usual wild boasts, only I was in the saloon at the time, playin cards, and I overheard him.

So why didn't he kill you on the spot?

Because he didn't know what I looked like, and there was a dozen young men in the saloon, and none of em looked like an outlaw.

So you gunned him down in cold blood?

It wasn't like that. Texas Red was a walkin powder keg. And that night he'd already drained several cups of tarantula juice.

Tarantula juice?

Chain lightning.

Chain lightning?

Bravemakers.

Bravemakers?

Whiskey, son, whiskey. And now, enlivened by all that tarantula juice, he crosses from the bar to the swingin doors and fires his ivory-handled revolver three times into the night, shoutin that Billy the Kid's luck just ran out, and call the undertaker because Billy the Kid won't see the mornin sun, and remarks of that nature.

So what did you do?

Well, after he fires his three shots, I fold my cards at the poker table. I walk over to the swingin doors, and I say to Texas Red it would be a sight indeed to see the Kid gunned down right here in the saloon, and Texas Red says to stick around then, it's sure to happen. And I express admiration for his ivory-handled revolver, and he draws it from his holster and gives it over.

So that's when you shoot him?

Wait, Tommy, let me finish. As I turn the gun over in my hands, I open the cylinder and rotate it to make sure the hammer falls on an empty chamber when the trigger is pulled. And I return the gun. And I ask Texas Red again what he would do if the Kid showed his face in these parts, and Texas Red, ripenin into a state of high idiocy, says he would first shoot the Kid's right hand and then shoot the Kid's left leg and when he had him wounded and crawlin on the floor like a crippled animal, he would shoot him twice in the head, once out of pity and once out of kindness. I thank him for the description and turn to the entrance, and I say, without lookin back, adios Texas Red, and by the way my name is Billy the Kid. And as I push open the swingin doors, I hear the click of the empty chamber behind me. And then—

And then you spin around.

And then I spin around and fall to business.

Tommy's widely opened eyes danced with delight. You shot him dead!

A man cannot escape the demands of his destiny.

You shot him dead!

That I did, Tommy, that I did.

And I read you shot three bullets into his chin in as tight a groupin as anyone ever saw. And that's because he said he wasn't the type to take it on the chin.

Somethin like that.

How'd it feel?

How did what feel?

Killin a man like that, killin him right in front of you, how'd it feel?

We'll save that for another time, Billy said.

Tommy's voice rose higher with excitement. And you killed eight men after that!

Yes, I did, but not all at once.

And you gave it all up?

I did.

Didn't you ever want to shoot again? I mean, even after you made the deal with Pat Garrett and all?

Yes, I did, Tommy.

So did you? Shoot again?

No, I didn't. Not ever.

How could you stop yourself?

I just did.

What stopped you? Love? Marriage?

Billy let out a laugh. No, that's not what stopped me.

So what stopped you?

Like I said, Tommy, we'll save that for another time.

Billy took his foot off the running board, opened the door and folded himself into the car, bringing the interview to a close. As Billy's Model T drifted away, a Model A almost clipped him before braking in front of Tommy. Frank's stare from the driver's window drew Tommy over.

Where did you get the car, Pa?

Never mind that. You go to school?

Tommy held up his books as evidence.

Who was that man I just saw you with?

Billy the Kid.

What?

Billy the Kid, the outlaw.

Billy the Kid is dead. Everyone knows that.

No, that was him, Pa.

Stay away from that man, you hear?

Yes, Pa.

Frank looked at the darkening sun, almost effaced by the dust. Better take cover, son, he said. Wrenching the car into reverse, he backed up, changed gears and sped away.

NINE

illy was back in his hotel room when the dust storm came. He had lined the window with rags, but he wasn't worried. A dust storm in Pueblo was not the same as a dust storm in Oklahoma. A month earlier he had gone to the outskirts of Tulsa, and there he had experienced an Oklahoma dust storm firsthand. He had gone there to meet a man who was selling a diary, purportedly written by Billy the Kid. The diary, he knew, was an audacious forgery, but he wanted to read it and meet the man who had written it. The seller of the diary, it turned out, worked in a hardware store. He had limp colorless hair, deep-set eyes, a flat nose, with the only dimensional feature to his face being two incisors that overerupted, which, combined with his other features, made him look like an apathetic vampire.

The diary was a mishmash of all the dime-store novels ever written about Billy the Kid. What set the book apart from the others was that Billy the Kid was spelled as Billy Kidd. Evidently the author was laboring under the impression that Billy was a direct descendant of the great British pirate Captain William Kidd, a genealogical note every other biographer had somehow failed to uncover.

It was when Billy was about to leave the man's bungalow that the dust storm hit. The storm was the worst Tulsa had ever seen. The storm was alive—it was a living sand creature, over ten thousand feet high, with a mouth as wide as the sky, and a hunger that could not be sated. In a matter of seconds the sand creature was devouring everything that passed into its maw—cars, houses, buildings, telephone poles. Oklahoma dust, Billy discovered that afternoon, had magical properties. It slid under windows lined with newspapers and rags. It became small enough to penetrate clothing. It became large enough to clog the motors of cars. It levitated small objects and transported them to different streets or different towns or different dimensions. With supernatural sleight-of-hand, dust appeared beneath flipped-over dinner plates. Making itself invisible, it darted inside coat pockets, crept inside sock drawers and materialized in small heaps under claw-foot bathtubs that crouched behind closed bathroom doors. The storm that held Billy hostage was full of a biting resentment from the over-tilled land. It flung drifts of dirt against the front and back doors of farmhouses so the families couldn't get out. It suffocated and entombed any livestock it happened to catch in the fields. And now it caked the bandana that stretched around Billy's nose and mouth as he left the bungalow to move his car into the garage. Unable to breathe through the bandana, he removed it, and the dust stung his face. He cried out, and the venomous sand creature flew to the back of his throat and tried to choke him to death. The next five hours Billy spent inside his car, which wouldn't start, waiting for the storm to abate just enough so he could rush back into the bungalow. At a lull in the storm he jumped out of the car but had covered only a few yards when a curtain of dust rang down from the sky, and the bungalow vanished from sight. Spinning around, he found his car had likewise vanished. With bowed head, he inched his way forward in what he thought was the direction of the bungalow, only to find himself in the middle of the street with the storm shrieking around him on all sides. And there he stood, not knowing which way to go, his slitted eyes tearing in the corners, his breath filtering coarsely through his bandana. He had lost all hope he would survive the storm when the bungalow appeared twenty yards in the distance. Rushing to the door, he flung himself inside and spent the rest of the day and night locked in a bedroom with the hardware man, his wife and her asthmatic mother. Only the following afternoon, after the dust storm had coated every inch of Tulsa with the dry dust of its innards and departed, did Billy himself depart.

The storm that was rolling into Pueblo this afternoon had already spent most of its fury. Dust storms in Pueblo were a distraction, on the order of a general nuisance, and sometimes they were even entertainment, like when a hat blew off one man's head to land on another's, or when the front page of a Colorado Springs newspaper gusted from the sky into your open hand. It was the wake of the dust storm, its trailing beauty, that everyone waited for. Before taking its road-show to the next town, the dust storm flung sparkling granules of sand across the sky, and with the glow of the falling sun those granules became ropes of rubies, clusters of emeralds, and pyramids of pink and gold sapphires, and what were once the riches of the earth became the heaped-up riches of the sky.

As the storm whirled outside his hotel room, Billy raised his head only once to acknowledge it . He was writing again, and there was a melody flowing from his pen, and he must let it flow. His book, when it was published, would be the most accurate account of Billy the Kid ever written.

After the storm was gone, he ventured outside to the sidewalk where he joined other residents and guests of the Congress Hotel. Across the street a number of townsfolk were gathering. On an intuition Billy turned around and looked up. Grace was at the window of her room, the window pushed up, her eyes lifted to the sky. Billy turned his gaze back to the townsfolk. Every neck was craning to the sky, every eye exulting in the sky's jeweled magnificence, with no words spoken or needed to be spoken, and only after darkness descended did they separate.

TEN

L ater that night, a man in a canary yellow suit entered the Congress Hotel and spread his hands flat on the reception desk. He was black-skinned and in his sixties, and his smile was like a night full of stars and that was owing to his four front teeth that were made of gold and embedded with diamonds.

The night clerk behind the desk lifted hands that were enmeshed in string and spoke through the triangular opening of a cat's cradle. You want to see Dr. McCarty? Oh, you mean Billy the Kid. Room 14, second floor.

The man thanked him and pressed his lips together, and the stars in his mouth winked out.

A minute later Billy was answering a rap on his door when *Auld Lang Syne* burst upon his ears. After two verses Billy was still stumped. He had taken a full accounting of the face and figure before him and could not find a familiar feature. The man in the canary yellow suit paused, trying to remember the rest of the words, and in pausing, grinned, revealing the treasure in his mouth.

Why, if it ain't Charlie Peck, Billy said.

Peck's face was radiant. He picked up Billy in a crushing hug and popped him back out to the floor. Billy's eyes traveled from Peck's swelling shoulder pads down to his two-tone shoes.

Beats wearin a uniform for Uncle Sam, Peck said with a deep-throated laugh. Rolling his tongue over the galaxy in his mouth: So where can I get a cup o' kindness in this town? I brought my tuxedo.

Less than half an hour later the two men were crossing the street toward the speakeasy. The evening air was making an effort to be cordial, and Billy was feeling only a little warm in his tuxedo. Peck slowed his stride to accommodate Billy's shambling gait.

Clerk at the desk called you Billy the Kid. You still workin that angle?

It sure helped with the dentist trade.

At the unpainted door of the speakeasy, Billy gave a rap and another rap. There was no response. Peck gave him a puzzled look.

Never been here before?

Drinkin was never my sport, Billy said.

Peck stepped forward and knuckled out a merry rhythm and embellished it and extended it until the slat flew open, revealing two bloodshot eyes in the Judas hole. There was the sound of a sliding bolt, the thick-paneled door swung open, and from a fan-driven breeze came a mist of nicotine.

Stepping outside the building was Stokes, his black tuxedo absorbing all the light from the hallway. Hands on his hips, he gave Billy a long appraising look: Well, if it ain't the outlaw himself. Leaning back, he motioned to an unseen figure who revealed himself to be the sweating doorman. Take a look at Billy the Kid, fastest gun in the West.

The doorman was patting his damp forehead with a handkerchief. Billy he regarded with indifference.

Stokes shifted his gaze to Peck. And who might be this dusky saddle tramp?

Billy put an arm around his friend's shoulder. This here's Charlie Peck.

Stokes turned his head around and called down the hallway. Jimmy, we got a famous dead outlaw here and his friend Charlie Peck. Table twenty-six.

Turning back to Billy, Stokes dipped his frame so impossibly low that his brilliantined hair was only a foot from the ground. From this perilous pose he said in a grandiloquent whisper: Gentlemen, we are graced by your company.

Through a dimly lit hallway Billy and Peck followed Jimmy, a short man with a ruddy complexion and the rolling gait of a sailor on leave. Billy didn't know what he was expecting to find, but he had heard about the Cotton Club in Harlem with its potted palms, jungle murals, and barbarous drums that summoned bare-breasted girls in grass skirts.

The brick-walled space they entered was not a jungle, but here was savagery of another kind: men unbridling themselves with quart bottles of gin, men at crap tables throwing money away as if it were diseased, men dancing drunkenly on the dance floor with women rouged like harlequins, whose ample figures were amplified still further by the beveled mirrors on the walls. Some men were sitting with their wives or lady friends, and these men were the worst behaved of all, hollering to each other over several tables.

As Jimmy led the way along a planked floor, Billy shook hands with friends at each elbow: on his left, Pal Lass, Snook Timson, Alf Squyres and Milt Toohy, and on his right, McBride and Sally-Anne

Redman, Reid Mackie and Sven Svenson. To the many hands he couldn't reach, he waved. Jimmy handed off his two charges to a chinless man, and the chinless man led them through drifting smoke to a table at the back. On the stage a songbird was singing *Ain't Misbehaving*, the Fats Waller hit. The songbird's dress was suggestively torn, but no one noticed, least of all the five men in the band, who had closed their eyes to all the misbehavior in the room to glide along the golden river of sound.

In ten minutes Billy and Peck had amassed as many empty shot glasses at their table. Two more shots they raised fraternally.

To the courageous 10th Cavalry, Billy said thickly.

To the Rough Riders who supported us, Peck said in a clear voice, hitching his chair a little closer.

Down went the drinks. Peck raised four fingers like a blind man, and a slender waitress delivered four more shots. He paid her and tucked an extra bill into her whale-boned bodice. The waitress, drunk herself, gave her best imitation of a wink and clacked away on her heels.

Billy's shoulders were bunched closer now, and he gave vent to his curiosity, asking Peck what brought him to these parts. Peck threw back another murderous shot and said John Barleycorn. Billy said his question was serious, and Peck said so was his answer—he was opening up a speakeasy at Second and Santa Fe. The carpenters had already begun.

Billy asked what he knew about speakeasies and Peck bellowed out the familiar refrain:

Mother makes brandy from cherries.
Pop distills whiskey and gin.

Sister sells wine from the grapes on our vine.
Good grief how the money rolls in!

This morning Stokes killed a bootlegger, Billy said.

Peck downed another shot and slammed the bottom of the glass on the table. Remember Pawnee Broadfoot and Johnny Johnson? Billy threw back a shot and nodded. Haven't seen either of em in years, but I remember they were good riflemen and good Rough Riders.

They're workin for me now, Peck said. Got operations in Grand Junction, Durango and Colorado Springs.

He slid a shot across the table. Billy caught it and downed it and put his elbows on the table and missed by two inches.

You're splificated, Peck said. All roostered up.

That I am, Billy said. Cock-a-doodle-doo.

Peck laughed his deep laugh and unwrapped a soda mint and held it out, and Billy took it and lobbed it at his open mouth and hit his cheek instead. From the tabletop he retrieved the mint and pinching it between his fingers, placed it inside his cheek.

On the stage the songbird cut short her trilling and handed the microphone to Stokes. *Tap, tap, tap* went the microphone. *Tap, tap, tap.* When all the eyes of the room had turned toward him, Stokes spoke in his lofty voice.

Ladies and gentlemen, it's our privilege tonight to have a livin legend among us, a man once believed dead, but who is now very much alive, Billy the Kid!

He threw his hand out toward Billy, and the band struck up a triumphant note. With an effort Billy got to his feet and took a bow to thunderous applause. Without warning a hand seized Billy's forearm. The chinless man was guiding him to an unknown destination over a floor that undulated with each step. Billy glanced over his shoulder. Glittering in the darkness was Peck's starry smile.

Over at the long mahogany bar the head bartender was ringing a copper bell and shouting to clear the bar, causing the startled patrons to retreat with their drinks. The chinless man navigated Billy past the staring faces and left him leaning against the rail of the bar. Billy rolled along the rail until his leg hit a stool and sat down. The drink thrust in front of him he ignored, and forgot he was ignoring it and tossed it back. To better orient himself, he swiveled around on his stool. Stokes was approaching, but stopped halfway, turned his back to him and flung out his arms to the room.

Ladies and gentlemen, they used to say Billy the Kid could ride a buckin bronco and shoot two silver dollars in the air. Well, tonight we've made it easy for him. All he has to do is stand on these two silver dollars.

He held up a silver dollar between the thumb and forefinger of each hand and turned and placed the coins in Jimmy's palm. Jimmy, swaying with the roll of the room, crouched down and positioned the coins on the floor with the exaggerated delicacy of a drunk.

All Billy the Kid has to do, announced Stokes, is stand on those two silver dollars and shoot this buckin bronco.

Striding over to the bar, he broke off a tiny wooden horse from a decoration and held it aloft for everyone to see. He tossed the wooden horse to a bartender who tossed it to a second bartender who tossed it to the head bartender who wedged it atop a shot glass at the far end of the counter.

And if Billy the Kid can shoot that buckin bronco, Stokes said, it's drinks on the house!

From a hip holster he drew a pistol and handed it to Billy. The chinless man helped Billy off the stool and steadied him on the undulating floor while Jimmy, still crouching down, adjusted Billy's boot heels until they covered the silver dollars. Jimmy looked up, nodded to Stokes and crept backwards like a crab.

Ladies and gentlemen, Stokes said, throwing his arms out wide, Billy the Kid will now demonstrate his extraordinary talent as a gunslinger!

Applause deafened Billy, upsetting what little equilibrium was left in his eardrums, and he teetered off the dollars. Jimmy scuttled forward in his crouching position and repositioned Billy's boot heels. Regaining his balance, Billy raised the trembling gun. The bartenders dropped below the counter, and a reverent hush fell over the room.

Feeling nauseous, Billy lowered the gun, and summoning his strength, raised it chest-high—and burped. From the crowd came hoots and guffaws, and he soon found himself joining in the gaiety. For a moment he forgot he had a gun in his hand. Stokes reached over and lifted Billy's arm. Once more Billy took aim. This time he cocked the gun and touched the trigger. Nothing happened.

It might help, Mr. Kid, if you release the safety, Stokes said loudly to the room.

Staccato bursts of laughter. Stokes came forward and released the safety and took a wide step to the side. Once more Billy raised the weighty gun. Holding his breath to steady his aim, he took a bead on the wooden horse and closed his trigger finger. The pistol gave a barking jump, and a rose blossomed at the end of the muzzle.

Three yards in front of him the bullet blew out a hole in the floor, and it did so just as Billy's body was pitching forward. Mercifully Billy's eyes were shut as he hit the floor, so he did not have to view the calamitous result of his marksmanship. But his ears had popped open with the blast, and now they were assaulted with braying laughter.

At once Peck was standing over him. He bent down and pried the pistol loose from Billy's hand. Pushing Billy's legs aside, he anchored his own boot heels on the silver dollars, raised the pistol and blew the wooden horse off the shot glass. No one moved. There was only the sound of the head bartender scraping bits of wood off the counter.

Spinning around, Peck addressed the staring faces in an even voice: Drinks on the house.

Two seconds, and the seated population of the room jumped to their feet as one person, and the mahogany bar receded behind the throng. In the midst of all the pandemonium Peck hauled Billy to his feet, hoisted him over his shoulder and carried him out the door.

Stokes had observed Peck's performance with his boot jacked against the bar. Now he dropped his boot to the floor, turned to the nearest bartender and ordered a Gin Rickey.

ELEVEN

A chorus of red-eyed sparrows sang the next morning into existence. But their concert went unheeded by Billy whose eyelids were still weighted down with the sediment of sleep. At noon there was a polite knock on his door. A woman's voice: If it's inconvenient.

Billy roused himself. Making his way to the sink, he shouted to give him just a minute. He turned on the tap, splashed cold water on his face, rinsed his mouth with cologne, combed his hair and beard with his fingers and observed he was still wearing his tuxedo shirt and pants. Wiping his hands on the starched shirt, he tore it off and buttoned himself into a shirt of blue and green checks. The voice coming through the door was more pronounced: I'll come back.

Billy opened the door. Grace, looking remarkably pretty in her mourning dress, had her hands clasped at her waist. Her eyes were filled with a liquid hope—for what exactly Billy couldn't fathom. Almost immediately her gaze withdrew from his face and shifted over his shoulder to his writing desk where her eyes sought out the individual titles of his books. Billy blocked her view as he moved closer to her in the hallway.

Grace's nose wrinkled. Ever seen that movie *Ten Nights in a Barroom*, Dr. McCarty?

I haven't, Mrs. O'Bannion. But just for the record, I'm planning to forego all barrooms for the next nine nights.

Grace gave him a smile. I came here in the hopes of your help, she said. I have a painting to hang.

I know somethin about em, Billy said.

Paintings?

Hangings.

Oh, of course you do. How many did you escape?

Two.

Only two?

Two not enough for you?

Oh, I like to think a man like you would have escaped half a dozen hangings, Grace said.

As they walked the length of the hallway, Billy breathed in the scent of lilacs and circulated it in his lungs as if to transfuse some essential part of her mystery into his blood.

How long have you been workin on your book? Grace said.

All my life I've been livin my book, Billy said. The writin part of it has been just about two years.

That makes sense, Grace said.

What makes sense? Billy said.

Two years ago I saw you takin notes with a red Rayovac pen in the front row of the Paramount Theater. King Vidor's *Billy the Kid* was playin for the first time.

To think she had noticed him back then. To think she had taken any interest in what he was doing. A wave of euphoria swept over him. They reached her door. Grace paused by the entrance, turned and gave him a scrutinizing look.

I remember in the movie Pat Garrett let Billy the Kid ride off into the sunset in a true Hollywood ending, Grace said. Is that where you got the idea that you were still alive?

It was the true ending to a true American story, ma'am.

I heard that in France the picture had a different ending, an ending where Garrett shoots the Kid dead.

I like the French people, but they don't know the West, Billy said.

I don't think that's the point, Grace said.

It's my point, Billy said.

Well, we can resume this discussion on another occasion. We've got a painting to hang today, don't we?

She opened her door, and Billy's eyes roamed the room. Her dead husband appeared in an unbroken panorama of photographs running from the windowsill to the side table to the dining room table. Patrick O'Bannion was first a tanned prospector with a sack of gold nuggets, then a timid groom, then a proud sheriff posing outside his jail. None of the black-and-white photographs had even a speck of dust, and Billy could tell the photographs were not there for mere decoration.

Grace conducted Billy over to a large painting that was propped against the wall, and he bent down for a better look. A long-bodied black convertible was curving along a road that plunged between two purple foothills. The front seat of the car was occupied by a man and a woman, their hair held down by hats.

It's a Vauxhall Speedster, Grace said. Patrick always wanted one, but on a sheriff's salary, well, you know.

Billy picked up the painting and held it shoulder-height against the wall.

A little higher, Grace said. That's right.

Billy put the painting back on the floor and took a hammer and two small nails from Grace's hand. Pounding the nails into the plaster, he noticed a green-checked gingham dress partly visible inside a closet. Almost at the same time Grace nudged the door closed with her shoulder and leaned back against it.

I liked the car's lines, Grace said. I think I wanted the car more than Patrick did. That's why I put in both the woman and the man.

Billy looked at her, astounded. You painted this?

A long time ago. I haven't picked up a brush since Patrick died.

Billy picked up the painting, hooked it onto the nails and took a step back to admire Grace's artistry. There was a moment of silence. Grace went to the front door and opened it, keeping her hand on the doorknob. Thank you for your help, Dr. McCarty.

Billy was crossing the floor when he paused at the side table and picked up an old program from the 1908 Colorado State Fair. He looked up at Grace.

1908?

Grace crimsoned, and Billy tiptoed back his remark. Didn't mean to pry, he said. He placed the program back on the table.

Grace took a breath and pressed her hands together as if to beg his indulgence. I was Miss Rodeo Colorado in 1908, she said. After laughing at her own admission, she continued: William Jennings Bryan was visitin the fair, stumpin to be President for the third time, and he presented me with a tiara and a large pink sash. Her face was glowing with the recollection.

William Jennings Bryan, Billy said. What was he like?

A smile formed on Grace's lips. All I remember was this huge cross of gold he wore around his neck. Which, if you think about it, I mean, really.

I will not help to crucify mankind on a cross of gold, Billy said, repeating Bryan's famous campaign slogan.

That's right. He was against the gold standard and wanted our country to have its currency backed by both silver and gold.

I remember, Billy said. And when he lost the election in '96, and McKinley chose the gold standard, the price of silver dropped.

And silver continued a choppy course until 1908, Grace said, and then the price plummeted, and all the silver mines in Colorado collapsed overnight. We lost a sizeable holding in Cripple Creek. Where were you in the summer of 1908, Dr. McCarty?

Billy glanced upward as if the scroll of his life were unspooling across the ceiling. Let's see, he said. The summer of '08, I believe I was bronco ridin for Buffalo Bill's Wild West Show and doin some dentistry on the side.

On animals or people? Grace's smaller dimple was winking.

Billy's eyes left the ceiling and rested on hers. On people, he said.

His right hand found the top of an upholstered chair and his first three fingers played Taps on the fabric as he spoke.

There was this one Lakota brave. He was part of the show, and he needed me to extract a wisdom tooth in his upper jaw that had partially erupted. So this brave, he sits on the chair, refuses to take the cocaine for the pain reduction, and instead sinks into a self-induced trance for about twenty minutes and never flinches while I extract the tooth, and when I finish, he gets up, thanks me and leaves, just like that, just as though we'd been havin a friendly smoke together.

Grace was twisting the toe plate of her shoe on the floorboard, and Billy took the hint.

I'd better be gettin back to my book, Mrs. O'Bannion.

When Grace spoke next, he had already crossed the threshold into the hallway.

Speakin of your book, Dr. McCarty, I couldn't help but see all those history books in your room. If you're writin about your days as a famous outlaw, why do you need all those books?

Billy stopped in the hallway and turned around. I don't need em. But I want to know what's been written so I can set the record straight.

I thought, perhaps, you had a bad memory for details.

No, ma'am, I have a detailed memory for bad things. It's all the good things I've forgotten. Who am I kiddin, I've forgotten the good and the bad.

I noticed you have a book on Jesse James. I thought you said you were Billy the Kid. The smaller dimple in her cheek was challenging him now.

I met Jesse James once and wanted to include him in my story.

Oh, did you pull his tooth out?

I met him when I was Billy the Kid.

What did he talk about?

I'll get my notes, Billy said, gesturing to his room.

Oh, that's all right. Just tell me what you remember.

Well, I met him one night in the summer of 1879, in the Old Adobe Hotel in Ojo Caliente.

Ojo Caliente?

Ojo Caliente, New Mexico Territory. I saw a gentleman sittin by himself with a deck of cards and I asked if I might join him, and he was most cordial.

Aren't all outlaws? Grace said, smiling.

Billy let the comment pass. I took a seat at his table and as we played, the gentleman introduced himself as Mr. Thomas Howard from Memphis, Tennessee. But I know how people speak who are from Memphis, and his tongue didn't draw out the vowels in the Memphis way.

Did you suspect his real identity? Grace said.

Not at that point, but I suspected somethin. And as soon as I saw the missing tip of his middle finger I knew who he was, and I knew the best way to draw him out was to tell him who I was.

That you were Billy the Kid.

That I was Billy the Kid.

And how did he respond?

He said he had Billy the Kid fixed as a much larger man.

So even famous outlaws suspect you're not who you say you are.

A smile curved Billy's lips momentarily, and he continued. I told him how I escaped the Silver City Jail and I described the jail to a T, and he said he'd been to Silver City once, and though he'd never been inside the jail, my description sounded about right. And that's when he told me his real name was Jesse Woodson James, and that he was originally from Missouri, and he had come to New Mexico Territory to see if he could find a new homestead for his family. I told him about some nice areas nearby and he said he would check em out. He asked me again if I was really Billy the Kid and I told him to place the joker card on the wall at the other end of the bar. He did, and I got up and pulled my pistol from my holster.

And you shot the card right through the middle, Grace said.

Billy flashed his straight teeth. Well, I did shoot it right through the middle, at that. And, anyway, Jesse laughed and said he reckoned I was Billy the Kid, after all.

Grace raised her chin. What proof is there Billy the Kid was even at that hotel at the same time as Jesse James?

You want proof?

If proof even exists.

I got proof. But this time you have to let me go back to my room.

All right.

Billy went to his room and came back with an old copy of the *Optic* that said James was staying at the Old Adobe Hotel for two nights in late July. Next Billy produced a police document charging the Kid with running an illegal gambling table on the same two days in the hotel.

Got em from a collector, Billy said. They're authentic.

I don't doubt that they are, Grace said. But none of this proves you're Billy the Kid.

No, ma'am, no document ever could.

Grace handed back the documents. Did Jesse James ever ask you to join his gang?

If he had, I might have. I was a real desperado back then.

Is that so, Grace said in a voice tinged with doubt. By the way, what color were his eyes?

How's that?

Jesse James, the color of his eyes.

Billy paused. I don't know that I remember. Maybe blue or green. I don't often recall a man's eyes.

They were crystal blue.

How do you know?

Because my husband passed Jesse James once on a street in Nashville, and my husband said once you saw Jesse's eyes you could never forget em.

Billy could hear the accusation in her voice. My attention wasn't focused on his eyes, he said, but on the ring he wore. Did your husband ever remark on Jesse's ring?

I don't believe he mentioned it.

Well, see, I would say any man who met Jesse James would never forget his ring.

And what was so special about his ring?

It was made from a nugget of gold. I asked Jesse if he got it from one of his bank robberies, and he said no, he found it among his father's possessions after his father died. It was the one remembrance he had from him. His father was a preacher who went out to California to preach glad tidings to the gold miners but caught the gold bug and exchanged his Bible for a mining pan and panned himself broke. Along the way he picked up the cholera and died in Hangtown Gold Camp.

I'm impressed by your knowledge of Jesse James, Grace said with an appeasing smile.

Billy wasn't finished yet. I told him my Pa also went to prospect in the hills, and he never came back neither.

Seems both of you had fathers who liked to live fast, Grace said.

Fast is in my blood, fast is in my bones.

Grace smiled at him and took a step back into the room and thanked Billy for the fast hanging. Billy gave a short laugh and said it was the only hanging he had ever enjoyed.

TWELVE

An hour later Billy was in Peck's Place, traversing sandy planks of yellow pine while Peck trailed his fingertips over a long oak countertop, nearly completed in a single day. Peck paused where the countertop ended and pointed to a raised platform under construction at the back of the room.

That's where I'm puttin my dancin girls, Peck said, shouting over the banging down of boards. Bringin em in from Sante Fe.

Behind them the floorboards echoed with the clomp clomp of boots. Don't think you'll be able to afford em, Mr. Peck, a voice said.

Peck spun on his heel.

Stokes was advancing toward him, blowing out a pungent ring of smoke from his cigar. Dancin girls, Stokes said, shaking his head. Good ones cost you money, bad ones cost you customers. And you got to get singers on top of it. That's why I say forget the dancin girls, stick to singers with good legs.

Too late for that, Mr. Stokes, Peck said, taking out his own cigar and pushing it in his mouth. The dancin girls are on their way.

I was thinkin you might want a partner, Mr. Peck.

A partner, Mr. Stokes?

Someone to supply your hooch, Mr. Peck.

Well, that would be fine, Mr. Stokes, exceptin I already got my hooch.

My stuff ain't cheap, but it's well protected. This is a rough town, Mr. Peck.

Gunslingers on every corner, Mr. Stokes.

Stokes let a circle of ash drop to the floor. What I'm sayin is.

I know what you're sayin, Mr. Stokes.

A ribbon of smoke unfurled from Stokes's handsome mouth, giving him the appearance of a matinee idol about to deliver a startling revelation at the end of the third act. After pausing for dramatic effect, he let drop a single word: Magazines.

Magazines, Mr. Stokes?

Magazines, Mr. Peck. It's got so I can't go to the crapper without one. So I'm readin this magazine, see, and it says men don't smile as much as women. And no one knows why. But I got it figured out. Want to know what I figured out, Mr. Peck?

What did you figure out, Mr. Stokes?

Men are never satisfied—size of their wife, size of their pecker, size of their wallet. Never satisfied. That's what I figured out, Mr. Peck.

Peck waited until the talking was done and swept his hand in a wide arc and struck a match against a post. Holding the fire to the end of his cigar, he puffed it into life and said: Mr. Stokes, in all that readin of yours, you ever come across Robbie Burns?

Who?

Robbie Burns, the poet.

Poet?

Peck sang out the verse: It's hardly in a body's power to keep, at times, from bein sour.

Stokes stared at Peck for a long moment. I like the sentiment, Mr. Peck, he said, with no improved temperament. Turning on his heel, he advanced toward the door in long measured strides.

Billy asked Peck when the Rough Riders were coming, and Peck said they were on their way, and Billy said the sooner the better.

∿

For the remainder of the day Billy sat at his writing desk in his room. Describing a gunfight, he used the old terms that were common among gunmen fifty years earlier. An armed man was a heeled man. A bullet was a lead plum. To fire a gun was to unravel some cartridges. To kill a man was to blow his lamp out.

Into the late watches of the night Billy wrote, letting his imagination venture where it would, and at once he was lost in a reverie, he was young once more, he was a young man, and he was riding a Smoky Black Palomino in the murk of night, the pony's hooves stirring the soft dust, the pony bought from an old Mescalero, so the hooves unshod, the pony's broad back never knowing a saddle, and with the swaying rhythm of the pony's head swayed his own head, swayed his own body, his canvas-trousered legs wearing down the pony's black coat just behind its withers, and riding with no tack except for a horsehair bridle bought from a trader and made from five thousand half-hitches by some forgotten cowboy in a Western jail with time hanging heavy on his hands, the dark blue *Lucky Me* fading across the brow piece, and Billy feeling lucky to be free, lucky to be living on this rolling earth, lucky to be breathing the scent of creosote bush and sagebrush made sharp by the night dew, the cool night air cooling the pony's head, cooling his head as they passed through the swimming darkness until the moon showed its face and splashed its glamour on the pony's neck, and taking the pony under the branches of a desert willow, and the dripping pony coming to a standstill, its hide a coat of diamonds through the lit branches, and sitting on the damp hide, and rubbing the pony's lathering neck, and listening for any other hoofbeats, but there were none, just the sound of him breathing and the pony breathing and the ancient sounds of the breathing night, and the moon hiding its face, and his heels not touching the pony's sides, and whispering to the pony the words he had learned from the old Mescalero, and the pony moving back to the darkened trail, softly stirring the dust with its hooves.

THIRTEEN

___

The next day, Billy returned from a meeting of the Spit 'n' Argue and stood in front of his hotel room, key in hand. On an intuition he pressed the door with his fingertips. The door yielded to his touch. His eyes flew to his two six-shooters that were out of their case and sprawled at odd angles on his writing desk. Stacked beside the guns were three schoolbooks. Without a sound he crossed to the closet, yanked it open—and accelerated Tommy to the floor. Red-faced and trembling, Tommy scrambled to his feet and in a torrent of words disencumbered his conscience.

School let out early. Took the spare key when the clerk wasn't lookin. Just wanted to see your Colt Double-Action Thunderers. Didn't mean for you to find me here. Please don't shoot me.

Billy crossed over to the guns and secured them in their felt outlines in the wooden case. Over his shoulder he said: People get thrown in jail for breakin into other people's homes.

I'd escape from jail. Climb up the chimney.

Silver City jail, Billy said, turning around. You read my manuscript.

Parts of it. Couldn't help it. It was right there on your desk beside *American Dentist*. And I was reading about your last escape where you had to shoot your way out. Did you really kill two deputies?

Yes, Tommy, I did.

Were they bad men?

One was bad, his name was Pecos Bob. The other, Deputy Bell, was more like a friend.

Tommy looked at Billy with curious eyes. You shot your friend?

Well, I did, but it's a bit of a story.

Tommy sat on the floor, locked his hands around his knees and waited.

Billy straightened the manuscript pages, turned around and leaned back against his desk. Well, as you know from what you read, Pecos Bob and Deputy Bell were guardin me in a cell on the second floor of the Lincoln County Courthouse.

And Pecos Bob had it in for you ever since you killed his friend in the Lincoln County War.

Well, that's what he always said, though I was not the one who killed his friend. Anyway, Pecos Bob shows me a brand new ten-gauge shotgun and says he hopes I'll try to escape so the shotgun can give a demonstration of its virtues.

So what happened? Tommy said, rocking back and forth.

Well, on the evening of my escape, Pecos Bob goes to dinner at a hotel across the street, takin five other prisoners with him and leaves Deputy Bell and me on the second floor. Now, I liked Deputy Bell. He was courteous to me. He was a courteous man. We were playin cards that night, the deputy and me, and all the while the Mexicans were singin outside the courthouse. I remember one of em had a four-stringed leona, carved from a single piece of cedar, another had a twelve-stringed bajo sexto, and there was a fellow with a violin carved in the shape of an eagle. And between the songs they would shout up to the windows, El Chivato! El Chivato!

Why were they shoutin that?

Because I gave em hope. Because I stood up to those who preyed on the weak.

So how'd you escape?

I'm gettin to that. First, I try to make a deal with the deputy. I tell him I consider myself a prisoner of war and like all good prisoners of war, I plan to escape and if he'll let me go, he'll be well rewarded.

And what does he say?

That he's a sworn officer of the law, and that as much as he likes me, he can't help me in this regard. So the die is cast.

How so? Tommy said.

Well, I'll tell you how so, Billy said. After the card game, Deputy Bell escorts me outside the building to the privy in the backyard of the courthouse, and when I come out, he leads me back inside the courthouse. Now, I'm in my leg irons, don't forget, and I'm hobblin up the stairs, one stair at a time, and always one stair ahead of the deputy. And all the while I'm thinkin in my head what I'll do when I reach the top stair, and when I reach the top stair I do it.

Do what?

Spin around and smash my wrist irons on his head.

You kill him?

No, he falls backwards against the wall and I pull his Colt from his holster. But he manages to get his hand on the barrel, and we have a tug of war, and I get my finger inside the trigger guard and I fire a shot. Well, the gun isn't aimed at him, but the bullet ricochets off the wall and goes straight into his gut. And down the stairs he tumbles until he crashes out the door, dead.

Tommy inhaled sharply.

So I hobble back up to the second floor, Billy said. I still had my wrist irons on, don't forget, and I have to get rid of em, so I use a trick I'd perfected when I was a teenager. Now watch this, Tommy, he said, stretching out his hands.

What are you doin?

It's called stretchin the bones. Houdini could do this, but not many others. So I stretch and stretch and stretch like this until the wrist irons fall off like giant bracelets.

Tommy's mouth opened.

I toss the wrist irons out the window, Billy said, and hobble in my leg shackles down the hallway to the armory. There's a Winchester in the rack, but I ignore it and grab Pecos Bob's new shotgun and move over to a window that overlooks the street.

You're waitin for Pecos Bob to come rushin out of the hotel on account of the gunfire.

Which is exactly what he does. And he runs over to the yard just below my window, and I level his own shotgun at him and shout out his name. And he reaches for his Colt.

And you kill him with his own shotgun!

That's right, Tommy, with his own shotgun. And with all the strength in my arms I slam his shotgun on the windowsill and break it into several pieces. And I toss the pieces outside on the ground.

Why'd you do that?

So his ghost would busy itself for eternity tryin to reassemble it.

Tommy's eyes grew wide. But wait, you still have the leg shackles on.

Good memory, Tommy. So I go back to the armory and take the Winchester and two Colt Double-Action Thunderers and a couple of ammunition belts and come back to the window and shout to the prison gardener to toss up a tool, and I reach my hand out the window and snatch a prospector's pick right out of the darkness, just like that, as if a floating storehouse of invisible goods was always available to me, I just have to reach out the window and take whatever I need. Within minutes I pry off the right ankle shackle, but the left shackle is welded differently, and I have no luck with it. So in one last affront to Pecos Bob I steal a piece of string from his desk and use it to tie the danglin bit of ankle chain to my belt.

I know the last bit of the story, Tommy said. Everyone does.

Suppose you tell it to me then.

The gardener, he brings out a horse that belongs to Billy Burt, who was a friend of yours, and you try to mount it, but the horse bucks you off because it's spooked by the ankle chain against its flank, and you have to mount the horse a second time, and the horse is all rearin and curvettin like, and you shout to the crowd: Adios, boys, tell Billy Burt I'll send his pony back. And don't look for me this side of Ireland!

That's all true what you said.

Tommy's face took on a look of worshipful awe. And I read in another book you were singin a song as you skinned off into the night. You had just killed two men and you—you were singin a song!

I wasn't singin as I rode into the night, Tommy. I was doin a chant.

A chant?

An Apache blessing, askin the Unseen to bless all of creation, a blessing that included me, my horse and the spirit of Deputy Bell.

The unseen?

With a capital U.

Billy pointed to the two guns on his desk. Those are the very same guns I took with me that night.

Tommy's eyes fastened on the Colt Double-Action Thunderers. Jumping to his feet, he moved closer to inspect them. How come they have tags?

I bought em at an auction.

Tommy's face looked tragic. They're not yours?

They are, but I sold all my guns after I stopped bein an outlaw. Needed the money for my dental practice. Two years ago I saw em at an auction and bought em back.

Reaching into his wallet, Billy took out a small newspaper clipping, heavily creased and folded, and handed it to Tommy. Read it, he said.

Tommy unfolded the clipping and read the words aloud.

BILLY THE KID.
$500 REWARD.

I WILL PAY $500 REWARD TO ANY PERSON
OR PERSONS WHO WILL CAPTURE
WILLIAM BONNY, ALIAS THE KID,
AND DELIVER HIM TO ANY SHERIFF OF
NEW MEXICO. SATISFACTORY PROOFS
OF IDENTITY WILL BE REQUIRED.
Lew. Wallace, Governor of New Mexico.

That notice, Tommy, was in every newspaper in New Mexico Territory.

Did you buy this notice at an auction too?

Cut it out of the Southwest Sentinel the first day it appeared. Been carryin it with me for fifty years.

Fifty years! Why'd you carry it around all that time?

First out of pride and later so my death would not go unnoticed. You can keep it.

You mean it?

I do mean it. And if you're short of cash someday, you can turn me in and get the reward.

No, I wouldn't. Not ever!

That was a joke, Tommy.

Which part?

Every part.

Billy turned back to the gun case, clamped the lid shut, took it over to the closet and placed it on a high shelf. Let's leave the guns up here from now on.

Can you twirl em on horseback? And shoot two silver dollars in the air?

Billy didn't answer. He went over to his writing desk and picked up Tommy's schoolbooks and handed them to the boy. So you like guns, do you?

When I get me some money, I'm goin to buy a Smith & Wesson hand-ejector.

Oh, a Smith & Wesson hand-ejector.

I know all about guns, Tommy said with conscious pride.

Oh, you know all about guns, do you, Tommy? Billy put on his hat and made his way to the door. All right, Tommy, let's see what you know about guns.

Tommy needed no second invitation. He rushed to the door and opened it before Billy's hand could reach the knob.

Fast, Billy said, nodding his approval. Fast is a big part of guns.

~

At the intersection of Fifth and Main, Billy and Tommy reclined against the wall of the bank. Billy told Tommy to pay fantastic heed to what he saw, and with a subtle movement of his head indicated a cowboy in bib overalls sauntering in their direction. Ten feet in front of them, the cowboy paused to talk to a friend. Billy whispered to Tommy to look at the wallet protruding from the cowboy's back pocket.

Just a wallet, nothing special, Tommy said quietly.

It's a wallet holster, Billy said.

How can you tell? Tommy said.

First clue is the rough leather on the outside. The rough leather keeps the holster from slidin around in his pocket. The smooth side of the leather is inside the wallet to give you a fast draw. The second clue is the hard line that runs down the side of the wallet, which is made by the barrel of a pocket pistol.

Tommy blinked his eyes in wonder.

The cowboy moved on, and Billy switched his gaze to a young Mexican male crossing the street. Tommy followed Billy's line of sight. Billy pointed out how the man's jacket bulged under his shoulder. Tommy asked what it meant, and Billy said it meant the jacket was covering his hide-out, his shoulder holster.

Billy's eyes shifted once again. The Stutz had just parked down the street. Stepping out of the car was Stokes's chauffeur. In his hand he had the funnies section. Snapping up the funnies to his eyes, he strode along the sidewalk.

How about him? Tommy said, looking at the chauffeur's uniform, which, loose in the cut, only emphasized the stringy body underneath.

You tell me, Billy said.

Tommy shrugged his shoulders. He had expended all his powers of observation.

Keep lookin, Billy said.

The chauffeur bumped into a woman. Dropping his newspaper, he stooped gracefully to retrieve it. Billy's voice lowered. Look how he bends at the knees, the way a lady bends to pick up somethin she's dropped. Means a gun at the hip. He's especially dangerous.

Why especially?

Hip draw is the fastest. And if he wants to be faster, he don't even draw.

Tommy looked at him for an explanation.

He shoots through the end of his holster, Billy said, and never draws his gun. In the old days we called those folks gun tippers.

A man emerged from the feed store. It was Stokes's doorman. His forehead was beaded with sweat and he had sweated through the back of his jacket.

What about him? Billy said.

His coat moves kind of like a pendulum, Tommy said.

Billy nodded. When a man moves slanchways like that, means he's got a fifteen-inch sawed-off shotgun strapped into a figure-eight, parallel to his body under his armpit.

Tommy gasped audibly.

Down the sidewalk there now came three well-dressed businessmen who were talking amongst themselves.

What do you think of em? Billy said.

Nothin unusual I can see, Tommy said. Are they clean?

They might be clean, Billy said, or there might be a pocket pistol up a sleeve, or a breaktop pistol in a hat or boot, or a belly pistol hidden in a waistband. No way to tell.

Tommy blew a whistling jet of air through his teeth.

A woman bustled past Tommy with a large purse. After she was out of earshot, Tommy said she might have a pocket pistol in her purse, and Billy said now Tommy was getting the picture. As Tommy's eyes combed the crowd, he bounced a little on his feet and pointed his forefinger.

Look over there. A gangster, a real gangster!

With his hand Billy lowered Tommy's finger and glanced at the gangster in question. A handsome man with brilliantined hair and a pencil-thin moustache was smoking a cigarette as he strolled along the sidewalk. In his free hand he gripped a hand machine gun as if it were a toy he had just purchased for a child. Billy did his best to suppress a smile.

Tommy, that's no gangster. That's Robin Hood.

Robin Hood?

Robin Hood from the movies. Douglas Fairbanks. He's a Colorado boy. Comes by here on his way back from Denver sometimes.

What's he doin with a Chicago typewriter in his hand?

He's been carryin one with him ever since the kidnappin threats against his wife Mary Pickford.

Why does he look so sad?

Mary Pickford and he just busted up.

So why is he still sportin around the gun?

Because once you start carryin a gun, Tommy, it becomes a part of you, and if you leave it behind, you've left part of yourself behind.

Why is he allowed to carry it in the open like that?

Like I said, Tommy, he's Robin Hood.

Before Tommy could ask another question, Frank's Model A pulled up, and Frank shouted for Tommy to get in the car. Tommy shouted back that he was only talking. Frank got out of the car, brushed past his son, marched over to Billy and asked if he was Billy the Kid.

Billy said he was. Frank nodded as if reassured, turned away, turned back and took a sudden swing at Billy. Billy jumped backwards, avoiding the blow, but lost his balance and windmilled all the way down until his head smashed against the sidewalk. Tommy cried out that Billy was hurt, and Frank told his son to get in the car.

On the sidewalk Billy lay, his head roaring. With the deep rumble of Frank's car the roaring in Billy's head got worse. As the sound of car grew fainter, a white-walled tire rolled up to the curb, inches from Billy's head.

The opening and shutting of the car door, the creak of leather boots, and two strong hands gripped Billy's armpits from underneath and lumbered him up to his feet. Peck was brushing down Billy's coat with his hands and saying Billy was down for the count longer than Gene Tunney. Billy said he still had his fast reflexes, just not his balance.

Feast your eyes, Peck said, turning Billy's body around. Feast your eyes.

Billy drew in his breath. Peck's car, painted a reflecting green, was an extraordinary sight to behold. It was a swaggering affront to every other car on the road with its many mirrored surfaces that could blind a pedestrian as easily as another driver, its multitude of floating lights that were a Milky Way of stars, its bulbous fenders that were the drooping leaves of a jungle plant, its two spare white-walls victoriously mounted on either side like captured trophies from beautiful dead cars.

Peck went over to the front left fender and pushed it down with his hand. Every Vauxhall Speedster comes with absorbers for shock, he said.

What kind of car did you say this was? Billy said.

Vauxhall Speedster.

Well, I'll be damned.

Just picked it up today.

Well, I'll be damned.

Peck opened the driver's door and made a magnanimous gesture with his hand. Billy lowered himself inside, sinking into the plump red leather and feeling with his fingertips the smooth wood panel-ing that encased him. This was no car he was sitting in, this was an elaborate piece of furniture. Peck leaned over Billy's shoulder and pointed to the dash. They call this the speed-o-meter, he said. Tells you how fast you're goin. He pulled a knob, and two windshield wipers rasped across the glass. For when it rains! he said.

Billy gripped the steering wheel in his hands and closed his eyes and inhaled the scent of hot red leather, distilled by the sun. It was the same scent he had tried to imagine when he looked at the painting in Grace's room.

FOURTEEN

Not five minutes later the Vauxhall was crunching pebbles in a slow parade down the street, and Billy, at the wheel, was waiting for Grace O'Bannion to look over from the sidewalk with astonished eyes. But after one disinterested glance, she kept to her course.

It's a Vauxhall Speedster, Billy said.

I know what kind of car it is, Dr. McCarty, Grace said, her gaze fixed straight ahead. Women in mourning do not joy-ride.

We can take the back roads.

That would be worse.

I only have it for an hour.

Grace paused and twirled her body toward him. May I drive?

I don't think my friend would mind, Billy said.

He helped her into the driver's seat and walked around to the passenger side. He was about to open the door when the car surged forward and tore down the street. With the car's increasing speed came a cry of wild excitement from the driver. After a hundred yards Grace executed a perfect one-point turnaround, throwing up a roostertail of dirt and gravel, and streaked back, braking to a hard stop in front of Billy. Dismounting from the car, she lifted her chin in casual triumph, swept aside an errant lock of hair, said thank you and resumed her stroll along the sidewalk.

For several seconds Billy watched her walk away, then slid behind the wheel and took the car in the opposite direction. Traveling through the center of town, he pressed on the horn to hear the sound, and out came the mating call of an African elephant. Heads turned in his direction, and he waved. In front of Peck's Place he pulled up and glanced across the street. The Stutz was parked there. The chauffeur was hanging his buck teeth over his lower lip, and the doorman was sitting beside him, his face glistening. They were keeping their eyes employed as two workmen carried a large cowboy painting through the doors of Peck's saloon.

Billy had not taken five steps toward the saloon when the barrel of a gun dug into his left temple. He let his arms fall loose by his sides and waited for the voice to come in his ear, and when it came, it was low and menacing. Where's Peck?

Billy said nothing. His right temple indented with a second barrel.

You were drivin Peck's car, a second voice said. Where is he?

I got fast reflexes, fellas, Billy said. Better holster those guns.

Who do you think you are? the first voice said. Billy the Kid?

As a matter of fact, I am Billy the Kid.

A pause followed, and both barrels lifted from Billy's head. A hand spun Billy around, and the first man hugged him mightily, reeled him off to the second man who hugged him mightily who reeled him back to the first man who gave an even mightier hug who reeled him back to the second man who so knocked the wind out of Billy with the mightiest of mighty hugs that Billy suspected the two men had decided to kill him not by a bullet to his brain but by squeezing the oxygen out of his lungs.

His body finally coming to a rest, Billy got a look at the two men. The first was a full blood with flowing silver hair and a long scar dragging across his left cheek. The second was a deeply tanned white man with lambchop sideburns and a black pirate patch over his right eye. Both men were grinning as if they were conspirators in a great jest. Billy stared at the men blankly, and all at once his eyes grew bright.

Pawnee Broadfoot! Johnny Johnson!

Pawnee Broadfoot let out a war whoop, and Johnny Johnson danced a jig on the spot. Rough Riders they had been, Rough Riders they would always be.

From the saloon came an exuberant shout: Welcome to Peck's Place, boys!

Peck was standing at the entrance, a fresh cigar in his mouth. He cocked his head to the side and shouted to the bartender, and by the time Billy had mounted the steps with the Rough Riders, a tray of brimming shot glasses greeted the men. Pushing through the swinging doors, Billy cast a glance around the saloon. Much progress had been made in a short amount of time. The long bar had been completed, as had the raised platform for the dancing girls, and the workmen were now hanging tin chandeliers from the ceiling.

Billy turned to Peck. How long have Stokes's men been out there?

Over an hour. Peck turned to the bar. Broadfoot! Johnson!

The Rough Riders were refilling their shots. They wheeled at Peck's call and strode over at once.

~

Peck was tapping on the driver's window of the Stutz. With an air of supreme apathy, the chauffeur lowered the window.

You boys look highly bored out here, Peck said, patting the roof of the car, so I thought I'd give you a little entertainment.

Turning around, he crossed the street in a spritely walk. When he reached the swinging doors of his saloon, he glanced up the street, and at a signal from his hand a bugling horn split the air. Over at the Stutz, the chauffeur and the doorman were elongating their necks to locate the source of the sound. The answer came in the shape of Peck's Vauxhall that was tearing down the street toward them with a stick of wood wedged in the wheel. Straddling the hood, with their pistols raised to the sky were the two Rough Riders. And now Pawnee Broadfoot, his silver hair lifting in the wind, arched his boot over the steering wheel and kicked life from the horn again.

At the saloon entrance Peck caught two beer bottles from the bartender, and turning to the street, hurled the bottles high into the air. The Rough Riders waited until the last possible moment before they blasted the bottles to pieces. As the Vauxhall was rushing past the Stutz, the two Rough Riders took mirrors from their pockets and holding them at arm's length, pointed their pistols over their shoulders and fired.

The crack of the pistols was instantly met with the sound of exploding tires. As the Stutz sank down on its haunches, the chauffeur started the engine, and the wounded beast limped away, dragging its carcass down the street.

Peck glanced at Billy. I want to enlist your services, Dr. McCarty.

Billy tugged at his beard. Peck, guns and me.

I was thinkin of your band. My dancin girls are muchachas. They'd go well with your music. Whatever they pay you at the cantina, we'll double it.

Well, I'll speak to the band about it.

The Vauxhall drew up to the saloon entrance. Pawnee Broadfoot was in the driver's seat, holding in his hand the large rock that had pressed against the accelerator. Johnny Johnson was lounging like a checkmark in the passenger seat with his boot heels dangling over the windshield.

Billy ambled over. Haven't seen nothin like that since Havana days.

Havana ain't never seen it neither, Johnny Johnson said with eyes of merriment.

No one seen it, Pawnee Broadfoot said. His smile was wide enough for Billy to glimpse a pegged upper right lateral incisor.

How about a lift home? Billy said.

Johnny Johnson swiveled in his seat and threw his body over the passenger door, landing in a standing position on the pavement. Billy climbed into the vacated seat as Johnny Johnson went clambering into the back. Pawnee Broadfoot gave the car some gas and the car glided into the street.

On their way to the Congress Hotel, Billy and the Rough Riders passed through an alleyway where ash-covered men shoveled mounds of ash into wheelbarrows. The ash came from the pits that smoldered behind the houses. Every morning the residents burned their trash in the pits, and every afternoon the ash-covered men removed the ashes. It was honest work, Billy thought, albeit low-paying, its chief virtue being no one ever got himself killed shoveling ashes. Pawnee Broadfoot cleared his throat and Billy turned toward him. The Rough Rider's face went rigid, and his long scar burrowed deeper into his cheek. He parted his lips, closed them and parted them again, the strange ritual persisting for two blocks.

What is it, Pawnee? Billy said.

How'd you know I wanted to say somethin?

Just a wild guess.

Well, as you know, I joined the Rough Riders late in the day. And I heard certain things about you, about your past and all. And at the end, we all went our separate ways.

And what you want to know is, am I really Billy the Kid?

Yes, sir, I mean, well, yes, sir.

The car had rounded a corner and was approaching the Congress Hotel. Pawnee Broadfoot shifted gears to give Billy more time to answer.

Did you hear they discovered a new planet two years ago? Billy said.

A new planet?

Pluto. It's called Pluto.

Can't say I ever heard of it.

You never heard of it, but it exists just the same, no matter who believes in it or not.

Pawnee Broadfoot reached the hotel and pulled up on the hand-brake. Billy thanked him for the lift and was starting for the hotel entrance when Johnny Johnson called out from the back seat.

Hey, Billy. Why you done it?

Billy paused in his footsteps and turned around. Done what, Johnny Johnson?

Johnny Johnson tilted his head back so his good eye could clear the brim of his hat. Why you done give it all up and become a toothpuller?

Johnny Johnson, you ever think of doin somethin else, other than bein on the wrong side?

At my age? The Rough Rider rubbed his nose up and down with the tips of his fingers.

You could join the Pinkertons.

That's the dentist in you talkin.

The dentist is still alive, Billy said. He started again for the hotel.

Hey, Johnny Johnson said.

Billy wheeled around.

Did you really ride a horse? Johnny Johnson said. Twirl your guns and hit two silver dollars in the air? I mean, that's impossible, ain't it?

El Chivato! came a strident voice from the hotel.

Billy turned in the direction of the voice. Gabriel was sitting on the steps to the entrance, a pillow sashed around his head. Billy turned quickly back to the car. It appears, Johnny Johnson, I got me a patient.

Johnny Johnson touched his forefinger to the brim of his hat, and Pawnee Broadfoot put the car into gear.

As Billy approached the hotel entrance, Gabriel tented his fingers and tipped his pillowed head to the side to make his plea more plangent.

El Chivato.

Gabriel, I told you before.

No, Billy, no voy a ir.

I sold all my instruments.

No me importa.

Gabriel got up and followed Billy inside the hotel. The day clerk was no longer playing cat's cradle. He had moved on to a game of his own device, fashioning a multi-layered pattern of string that employed all of his fingers and several toes of one foot. He lowered his foot as Billy approached the desk.

That's okay, Norton, Billy said. I just need to borrow some of this. He picked up the spool of string from the end of the counter.

This be for pleasure, Billy?

No, this be for pain.

In two minutes Gabriel was gripping the sides of a chair in the hallway, a string tied around his tooth, the pillow sashed even tighter around his head. He watched as Billy unraveled the spool of string in his hand, walking backwards across the hallway into the Palm Room. Billy closed the double doors until they were almost shut and wound the string around one of the inside doorknobs until the string was taut.

Uno, dos, tres, Billy said through the crack in the door and jerked the door wide open.

As the tooth sailed out of his mouth, Gabriel lifted several feet out of his chair. He clutched his jaw and stabbed his forefinger in the hole where the tooth once stood and rushed over to the large gilt mirror. Opening his mouth to confirm visually what he knew physically, he ripped the pillow from his head and dashed outside, shouting: Gracias, El Chivato! Gracias!

Billy was reeling in the skittering piece of bone when he spied Dr. Benton sneering at him from the staircase. And you have the nerve to call yourself a dentist!

Dr. Benton whirled around and mounted the staircase, taking care to stomp on each stair, and by the time he reached the landing, had shaken loose his false teeth.

FIFTEEN

In the early evening light Billy had leisure to examine his appearance in the full-length mirror of his room. If his face had weathered visibly with the passage of time, his teeth had survived wonderfully intact with no exposed tooth-root visible above the gum-line. A single gold filling, twenty years old, shone from a back molar, that was all.

The click-clack of heels. Billy went to his door and lowered his eye to the keyhole. At the end of the hallway Grace was taking her key from her purse. Billy straightened his posture and ran his fingers through his hair.

At the sound of Billy's door opening, Grace turned around.

Billy took a few steps forward and breathed in the lilac scent still hanging on the air. He cleared the catch in his throat.

Evening, Mrs. O'Bannion, he said, walking toward her.

Evening, Dr. McCarty.

I was wonderin, if you, that is, I was thinkin that, perhaps, see, there's a square dance tomorrow night, would you, well, what I'm sayin is, well, why don't you accompany me?

Grace's mouth fell open. If Billy had asked her to attend a witches' circle in the foothills under a full buck moon, she could not have been more astounded.

You do dance, don't you? Billy said, halting a few yards from her door. Or is the hoedown dress I saw in your closet only for costume parties?

Thank you for the invitation, Dr. McCarty, but I'm afraid I won't be able to make it. You see, tomorrow night is Amos 'n' Andy.

The pin tumblers clicked in her lock, and she shifted the door open with her hip.

Pardon me for sayin so, Mrs. O'Bannion, but spendin every night by yourself.

But I don't, you see. I have all my memories. Good night, Dr. McCarty.

Good night, Mrs. O'Bannion.

Back in his room, in an effort to revive his spirits, Billy took down the gun case and removed the two Colts. From another shelf he brought down his Hoppes Gun Cleaning Pack with its tubes of grease, ungrease and bottles of Nitro powder solvent Number 9, the best remover ever made for metal fouling and rust. It had been months since Billy had last attended to his guns. Never once had he fired them since their purchase, so there was no real need for cleaning them. And with Pueblo's arid climate, the guns didn't sweat in their gun cases, so they didn't even need to be wiped down. But for Billy, cleaning guns was a meditative pleasure, so with one of his old giveaway toothbrushes, he scrubbed down the first gun, always moving in the direction of the bullet. He considered whether it was more dangerous to be a gunfighter in the Old West, or a dentist in the Old West who catered to gunfighters. His thoughts turned to the dentist who taught him dentistry some fifty years ago. The dentist was from Cheyenne, Wyoming, and one of his patients was Clay Allison, the notorious outlaw from Waynesboro, Tennessee. On Allison's first visit the dentist extracted the wrong tooth, and the next day Allison returned and extracted one of the dentist's own teeth with a pair of flat-nosed pliers.

After Billy had finished cleaning both pistols, a sudden impulse seized him, and with a sharp tug he snapped off the auction tags. Positioning himself in front of the mirror in the classic gunfighter stance, he thrust his trigger fingers through the trigger guards of both pistols and twirled them in opposite directions. For a single shining moment he was Billy the Kid, until one of the pistols flew off his finger, and he was Dr. McCarty again. Billy frowned. The pistol had crashed into the mirror, cracking it with the worse kind of bad luck.

As he stooped to pick up the pistol, a knock sounded on the door. Billy put the pistols back in the case and closed the lid. Change your mind? he said, opening the door.

His nose was greeted not with the scent of lilac this time, but with the aggressive fumes of a cigar.

Good evenin, Stokes said.

Good evenin.

I want to talk, private like.

This is as private as it gets.

Stokes had one hand on the doorjamb and was running his thumb along the groove like an engineer. You got to see it from my angle. I put a lot of money into my operation. Your friend comes along, opens up another club and wants to take my business away. I offer him a partnership, and he outright refuses me.

You're talkin to the wrong person. I'm not a businessman. Now, if you'll excuse me, I have work to do.

Taking a step back into his room, he gave the door a shove, but Stokes stopped the door with his shoe.

One other thing, Stokes said. I hear you're the best dentist for a hundred miles.

Was. I've retired.

Stokes reached into his mouth and clicked his two upper front teeth back and forth. Garbling his words over his fingers, he said: See how they wobble?

A sucking sound was followed by a short snap, and he pulled out a dental plate from which were suspended two front teeth. Billy took the maxillary plate in his hand and turned it over, admiring the craftsmanship. Well, I'll be, Billy said. A partial denture and a ceramic rotational path. And it's removable. I've read about these. First one I've ever seen outside a magazine.

Billy pressed his thumb on the spongy base of the dental plate. Looks like methyl methacrylate resin. You're a regular showcase for dental innovation, Mr. Stokes.

Better than the wooden dentures George Washington had, Stokes said, hissing the TH and whistling the S in a voice no longer his own.

Washington's dentures were made of all kinds of things, Billy said. Ivory, gold, human teeth, hippopotamus, but not wood. Billy wiggled the ceramic teeth of the dental plate with his forefinger. I have a small hammer inside. See what I can do.

Stokes grabbed Billy's forearm. Why did George Washington lose all his teeth? he said, as if solving the mystery behind the president's bad teeth might somehow shed light on his own predicament.

He lived on almost nothin but chocolate, Billy said. Used to order fifty pounds at a time. And he brushed infrequently, if at all.

Billy disappeared inside his room with the dental plate. Stokes took a step inside and called after him: You have a magazine I can read while I'm waitin? I'm a reader, you know.

At his writing desk, Billy shifted some books aside and located an old copy of *American Dentist*. Crossing back to the door, he presented the magazine to Stokes and said the waiting room was in the hallway.

Stokes gave him an amused look and backed into the hallway, and Billy closed the door fully this time. Through the door he could hear Stokes rifling the pages of the magazine and talking to himself. No, not talking, he was reading aloud, with hisses and whistles in his speech. Older people have more tooth decay than any other group, the voice began. A pause followed and the voice continued. Older people produce less saliva, and saliva cleans the teeth. With age, gums shrink, exposin the teeth to infection. A lot of older people have poor vision and mobility problems with their arms and hands, and this results in less effective brushing, which, in turn, produces more decay and infection.

Back at his desk, Billy knocked the teeth into the correct position. Through the door he could still hear Stokes reading, this time about gum disease and teeth breaking off and the problem with poor fitting dentures. When Billy opened the door and came into the hallway, Stokes held up his hand to finish the last sentence: These are the dentures that try men's souls.

Billy handed back the dental plate. This should keep until you get old.

Stokes snapped the plate in, and his smooth voice returned: Rather be dead than old.

That's what I used to say, Billy said.

But you're old now, Stokes said.

Yeah, always been unlucky.

Stokes pulled his lips back in a smile. The plate was well-fitted. So what's it like bein old? Stokes said.

Billy paused. The physical part annoys you, but it's the movies that destroy you.

The movies?

In your head. The movies in your head.

What movies?

From all your memories, Billy said. You play em over and over again until you spend more time livin in the movies than livin in the real world.

The light of reflection shone in Stokes's eyes. Them movies in your head, how do you stop em?

Just realize they're movies, not real, not worthy of your attention, and eventually they stop playin of their own accord.

The light left Stokes's eyes. I like livin in the movies in my head. Most people do.

You're got some strange ideas for a dentist.

That's what the other dentists used to say.

You should meet my friend Plato, Stokes said. He's a philosopher. Has a lot of strange ideas himself. Indicating the magazine: Mind if I borrow this? It was just gettin good.

It's yours to keep, Billy said.

∼

That night, at Peck's Place, Billy and his band played La Cucaracha while the Mexican dancing girls swished and swirled about the stage. The saloon was well attended. Many of the faces Billy had seen previously at Stokes's. Others were first-timers, men and women who wanted a more salubrious watering hole than what Stokes could provide.

Glancing up from his guitar, Billy observed Stokes enter the saloon, hat in hand. From a tin chandelier a light bounced on Stokes's head, making a triangular shape that gave him the appearance of wearing a lopsided crown. Peck was striding over, flicking his eyes sideways at Johnny Johnson who was positioned at the bar. Responding to the signal, Johnny Johnson slipped his hand inside his tuxedo jacket and kept it there.

Peck extended his hand to Stokes, and Stokes shook it. I take it back about the dancin girls, Mr. Peck. They're a nice touch.

Peck nodded, withdrawing his hand. Thank you, Mr. Stokes.

Mr. Peck, I'm votin against this Franklin Delano Roosevelt.

Why's that, Mr. Stokes?

Says he wants to repeal Prohibition. I don't need competition. I need cooperation. You should have cooperated with me, Mr. Peck.

Peck didn't have time to respond. The next instant the saloon doors crashed open, and hurtling inside came the sheriff and his two deputies. The sheriff fired his pistol in the air, blowing a hole in the ceiling, and all the sound escaped the room as if sucked up into the night.

Party's over for tonight, the sheriff said to the room.

The patrons took one long regretful breath. One by one they filed through the swinging doors that the deputies held open for them. The deputies said good night to Stokes, good night to Hal

Hardy the judge, good night to Reuben Bloom the school principal, good night to Clem Barstow the Presbyterian minister, and good night to anyone else who looked them in the eye. Finally the band packed up and left, leaving Billy alone on the stage, restringing his guitar.

The sheriff deposited himself on a stool and tapped for a whiskey from the bartender. The bartender measured out a generous number of fingers and did the same for Peck. Resting his forearms on the counter, Peck asked the sheriff how often he planned to conduct the raids.

The sheriff took a grave swallow of whiskey. Every night, he said.

Peck swished some bills off a roll.

Once a week, the sheriff said.

More bills floated onto the counter.

Once a month, the sheriff said.

Another layer of bills floated down and covered the first.

Once a month, with a warning, the sheriff said.

How often you raid Stokes's place? Peck said.

The sheriff glanced at Peck with a raised eyebrow. That's where I drink.

Billy passed by the two men, his guitar strapped upside-down on his back. He said good night to the men, and they said good night back, and Billy pushed through the swinging doors and left the two men sitting on their stools and drinking into the night.

～

Shortly thereafter, Billy was climbing the hotel stairs to his room when he noticed the orange light reflected under Grace's door. He moved down the hallway to his room as quickly as he could. He fumbled the key onto the floor, picked it up and glanced back at Grace's room. The orange light was still visible. Opening his door at last, he went over to his desk, pulled the desk chair over to the door, took the guitar off his back and sat down with his guitar in his lap. With the dim light from the hallway illuminating the strings, he strummed his guitar and sang a love song he had written many years ago, a song that was now about Grace. At the end of the second verse, the light under Grace's door went out. Billy took a deep breath and pushed the door shut with his boot and finished singing his song in the dark.

SIXTEEN

t noon the next day a group of men in the diner were crowded around a rectangular machine with a sloping glass top. A truck driver from Texas fed a buffalo nickel into a metal slot, pulled back the plunger, and the silver ball went shooting up the narrow passageway and made an arc under the glass before careening to the side, where it bounced against a rail and struck a cluster of silver-belled pins.

Billy and Peck were sitting with their backs against the counter, watching the men exclaim every time a pin was struck. Rosa flipped over Billy's cup and splashed in some coffee.

They call it a pinball machine, she said. I call it a livin hell.

The bell above the door tinkled as Grace entered, but the sound was lost in the ringing bells of the machine. Oblivious to the discord behind her, Grace crossed toward Billy. Dr. McCarty, I heard you singin last night. It was late.

Billy slid off his stool and stood up. Sorry if I disturbed you, Mrs. O'Bannion.

She gave a half-smile and her dimples appeared. On the contrary. How did an outlaw ever become so talented?

Peck rotated on his stool and touched Rosa's hand to stop the coffee overflowing in his cup.

Mrs. O'Bannion, Billy said, this here's Charlie Peck, an old friend. Charlie, this is Mrs. O'Bannion.

Peck planted his feet on the floor and brought up his body straight as a rifle. I was in the 10th Cavalry, ma'am. The 10th Cavalry landed in Cuba first. Teddy Roosevelt and his Rough Riders came after.

Grace searched Billy's face for an explanation.

I was with the Rough Riders, Billy said. Peck and the 10th Cavalry got to Cuba before me. Still, he's powerfully indebted to me.

Grace looked at Peck. Let me guess, he saved your life.

Not exactly, ma'am. He saved my tooth.

Peck opened his mouth and pointed to a lower right bicuspid, and Grace saw the aggregation of wealth in his mouth.

And did he shower you with gold and diamonds?

No, ma'am. I got the work done by a jeweler. Fourth tooth was free.

Grace laughed, covering her mouth with her gloved hand. Nice to make your acquaintance, Mr. Peck. Over her shoulder: Rosa, I'm goin to take the booth.

She started for an empty booth at the back as Peck and Billy hoisted themselves back on their stools. Peck slapped the counter. Now that's the kind of woman you should take to your dance tonight.

She don't dance no more.

Damn shame.

Once more the bell shook above the door. This time it was Frank who entered. Peck nudged Billy's arm. He's my new driver, joined my operation this morning.

I know him.

You know him? Howdy, Frank.

Frank gave a nod and took a seat on the other side of Peck. Billy stared into space. You should think of your son, Frank, he said in a raised voice. Leavin Stokes and joinin the competition could get you killed. And where does that leave Tommy?

Mind your own business, why don't you? Frank said, peering at Billy behind Peck's back and retracting his lips to show his teeth. In an instant Billy saw where Tommy got his jumbled teeth from. You don't care, sir, about your own son?

I don't care about you, mister.

Peck held his hands out, side to side, ready to push against their foreheads. But there was no need for the precaution. Billy had already dropped off his stool and crossed to the door.

SEVENTEEN

O nce out of the diner Billy made for his Model T. As he reached the driver's door, he heard running footsteps and turned around. Tommy appeared beside him, taking rapid shallow breaths.

What happened to that promise? Billy said.

What promise?

The promise not to ditch school anymore.

I just want to know what it felt like.

What it felt like?

Killin all those folks. You said you would tell me.

This is not the time, Tommy. You should be in school right now. A gunfighter keeps his promise.

I just want to know what it felt like, Tommy said, his eyes erupting with pain.

Forget about that. What's eatin you?

Tommy lowered his head, and for a moment it looked as if he might cry. When he looked up again, his face was burning. Sometimes I get so balled up inside I just want to gun someone down.

What's goin on, Tommy?

Tommy responded with downcast eyes. I'm a dunce.

What are you talkin about?

I'm twelve years old, and Mrs. Wagner asked me to do some multiplying. Six times nine. I didn't know the answer. I'm a dunce.

How many fingers you got?

Ten, of course.

Give em here, Billy said.

Tommy held out his hands.

Okay, nine times two, Billy said. Put down your thumb and finger for the two. Now how many fingers left, including the other thumb?

Eight.

That's right, eight fingers, Billy said. Now count the fingers you have down, but not your thumb this time.

One. One finger down, I don't count my thumb, Tommy said.

One finger down, that's right. Now put the one beside the eight. It's the answer to your sum.

Eighteen!

Okay, try nine times three.

Tommy repeated Billy's instructions. For the number three he put his thumb and two fingers down, leaving seven fingers standing. Not counting the thumb that was down meant two fingers down. Put two beside the seven, the answer was twenty-seven. Billy ran him through nine times four, and nine times five. Tommy counted his fingers and got it right each time.

You okay, mister? It was the sheriff shouting from his car, and he was addressing a stranger standing in the middle of the street. Lightly built, with even features and a blue jaw, the stranger was staggering about the street like an unhived bee drunk on fermented nectar.

The sheriff, getting no response from the stranger, parked his car. He was just opening his door when the stranger drew a pistol from his waistband. Four shots the stranger fired, and four streetlights burst open like great hatching eggs, sending a hundred pieces of jagged shell to the street.

Put down your gun, the sheriff said, unholstering his weapon and taking aim at the stranger's back. Just then the Stutz rolled up beside the sheriff, and out of the rear window appeared Stokes's head.

I wouldn't if I was you, Sheriff. Even drunk, he's a better shot than any man I know.

The sheriff swiftly holstered his weapon. Oh, didn't know he was a friend of yours, Mr. Stokes.

Plato! Stokes shouted out the rear window.

In an instant the blue-jawed stranger spun around and dropped into a crouch with his pistol aimed directly at the car. At the sight of Stokes, Plato lowered his pistol and rose to his full height. Taking a step backwards to steady himself, he grinned.

Stokes gave a jerk of his thumb, and Plato stumbled toward him, swiftly chambering four more shells into his pistol. While lurching toward the car, he pointed his pistol behind his back and shot a single bullet that crashed into another streetlamp. As the fragments sprayed into the air, he continued lurching toward the car and with his arm held behind his back, blasted the fragments to even smaller pieces until the overheated air was fretted with snow. Stokes opened the back door and shifted over. Like a high diver, Plato pointed his hands together above his head and dove inside. The car rolled away with his feet dangling and bobbing outside the door.

Billy looked over at Tommy. Come on, I'll give you a lift to school.

I don't know about school.

Get in the car unless you want to teach your father how to multiply.

Huh?

Get in the car. He's comin out of that diner in nine-times-zero seconds.

Tommy ducked inside the car. The next instant Peck and Frank emerged from the diner. Peck crossed over to Billy, and Frank hied off in another direction.

We saw it all from the window, Peck said. What was all the shootin about?

Stokes brought in some muscle, Billy said.

Well, my boys could use a little exercise, Peck said.

Moments later Billy was driving toward the school with Tommy in the passenger seat. You really want to impress your teacher with some multiplication?

Another finger trick?

This one goes way beyond fingers. I'm talkin the eleven times table.

Everyone knows the eleven times table. Even me.

You don't know it the way I know it, Tommy.

~

Mrs. Wagner, Tommy's teacher, was peering over her spectacles as Billy came forward into the classroom and doffed his hat.

Sorry to intrude, Mrs. Wagner. Tommy here knows his nine times table backwards and forwards.

Dr. McCarty, what a pleasant surprise, she said, rising to her feet. Nice to see you again, Tommy.

Billy and Tommy shared a glance of significance, and Billy turned to Mrs. Wagner. I also taught Tommy his ten times table, and his eleven times table.

Dr. McCarty, everyone knows their ten times table and eleven times table. Tommy, you may take your seat.

Billy gave a nod to his apprentice. Tommy, try 11 x 23.

Tommy hesitated less than a second. That would be 253.

Now try 11 x 54.

That would be 594.

The students had just witnessed water spring from a rock, and they were in thrall to their new god.

Mrs. Wagner smiled patiently. Well done, Tommy. You may take your seat now.

Billy threw another question to Tommy: Try 11 x 435.

Tommy put his forefinger to his temple as if to push the start button. A pause followed while his brain cogitated the impossible sum. That would be 4,785.

The hoax had gone far enough for Mrs. Wagner. Tommy, what is 11 x 2,343?

Tommy swallowed. The students murmured among themselves. From the back of the classroom came a peal of high-pitched laughter from one of the gap-toothed twins. The laughter passed down the row like a disease to the girl in front, and the boy beside her sputtered humorously into his hand.

Mrs. Wagner glanced at the students to silence them and turned to Tommy. You may sit down now, Tommy.

From Tommy's expression, it was clear he hadn't heard her. His eyes were moving in their sockets as if they were scanning figures on an invisible chalkboard.

Tommy, sit down, please, Mrs. Wagner said.

Tommy turned toward her. The answer is 25,773.

The room became quiet. Mrs. Wagner sat at her desk and did the sum under her breath, moving her pencil up and down the paper. Laying the pencil aside, she looked up. For pity's sake, Tommy, you're right.

No one had to tell Tommy to sit down anymore. He strolled, almost skipped down the aisle, threw himself in his seat, which skidded a couple of inches, and leaned back with his hands on top of his head like the laureled champion he was. The twins were silent now and looked on him with mouths agape.

Billy fitted his hat on his head and backed slowly toward the door. Sorry for the interruption, ma'am.

Someday you must tell me your secret, Dr. McCarty, Mrs. Wagner said.

I get asked that a lot, Billy said and left the room.

EIGHTEEN

A scented twilight entered Billy's room, bringing the soft shadows of romance, but for Billy romance would have to wait for another night. He adjusted the neckerchief ornamenting his neck, smoothed his hands over his fancy Western shirt and cinched his frontier pants one notch tighter with his silver-dollar belt buckle. Ready to greet the night, he sallied forth into the hallway.

At the top of the staircase he heard two men shouting inside Grace's room. For a moment he considered rushing down the hallway and breaking down Grace's door and rescuing Grace from whatever calamity had befallen her, but as the voices railed on, he recognized the familiar banter of Amos 'n' Andy, and his face broke into a smile. His thoughts still with Grace, he slid his hand down the banister of the staircase, and by the time her face had finally departed from his inner vision, he was descending the staircase to the church basement.

Billy opened the door to a whirling dance hall of high spirits and easy laughter. From the far corner the caller's voice was strong and resonant.

First couple out and circle four.

It's four hands all around the floor.

Stationed on the benches against the wall were a few old-timers bouncing their knees in time to the music. Whenever they lowered their gaze, the black specks swimming in their eyes transformed into bouncing black polka dots. These were the Heinz twins, who were wearing matching polka dot dresses. Their dichromatic parents had also brought along a Dalmatian, who sprawled on the floor.

On a platform in the far corner of the hall stood a fiddler sending a thumping rhythm into the air. A closer inspection of the fiddler's shirt revealed a gold star pinned below his left shoulder and a face that belonged to Jack Warden, the sheriff. Beside him was the caller, who not three hours earlier had worn the apron of a grocer. With a palsied hand the caller agitated the air and guided the dancers in a twangy monotone.

Birdie in the cage, it's three hands round.

Cage her in, go round and round.

Birdie hops out, the crow hops in.

It's three hands round and you're gone again.

Crow hops out, both couples swing.

Twirl around your pretty little thing.

From another part of the hall the druggist was threading his way through the dancers to the refreshment table. Approaching Billy, he shook his hand while darting his eyes around with the guilt of a criminal. What was Billy's view on prohibition the druggist wanted to know. Billy replied he was not what you would call a drinkin man. Upon hearing this, the druggist lost all poise and staggered about. His forced sobriety was ruining his natural equilibrium. Billy placed a gentle hand on his friend's shoulder and said in his view the government should have no say in a man's private life. In response, the druggist slapped jubilant arms against his sides.

Using Billy as a blind, the druggist removed a bottle of hooch from his jacket and leaned over the refreshment table, on which sat two punch bowls: one red, the other yellow. First he poured his hooch into the red punch bowl and placed a sign before it that said *Bad*. Next he placed a sign before the yellow punch bowl that said *Good*.

Billy watched as the druggist sampled a cup from the *Bad* bowl. Up came the cup and down went the punch. Three seconds passed. The druggist frowned as if to imply the punch had not lived up to its new reputation. Two more seconds, and his lips puckered, his left eye twitched and his body wriggled from head to toe as if he'd just swallowed a snake. Apparently dissatisfied with the results of this preliminary experiment, the druggist filled a second cup. Up came the cup, down went the punch, but this time his boot stamped repeatedly against the floor, suggesting a strong condemnation. Only a third cup, it seemed, could determine if the first two cups had been in error. Up came the cup, down went the punch. There was a pause, and the druggist shook his head with disfavor. But a moment later his boot struck the floor with such force that dust that had lain dormant for thirty years in the floorboards flew up in the air and formed a cloud around his head. Now, whether dust particles entered into his lungs at that very moment, or whether the

third cup had scorched the lining of his esophagus was impossible
to say, but the druggist coughed violently and refusing with his
hand the offer of a glass of water, threw back a fourth cup as the
obvious remedy. Turning red in the face, he gasped, ran in place
for several seconds with his knees up to his chest, gasped again and
grabbed Billy by both shoulders. That punch, the druggist said
gravely, is bad.

Billy was about to praise his discerning palate when a silky voice
whispered in his ear: *Dónde está tu novia?*

Billy turned around. Rosa, hands on her hips, wore an impish
smile.

Astonishment opened Billy's eyes as he lifted his gaze over Rosa's head.

My date, Rosa, has just arrived.

Rosa glanced behind her and put her hands up to her cheeks.
At the entrance stood Grace, flower-fresh in her green hoedown
dress. With a ballerina's weightlessness, she floated over.

Evenin, she said to Rosa, who lowered her hands from her
cheeks. To Billy: I changed my mind about your invitation, Dr.
McCarty. I do hope you don't mind.

I'll do my best to get over it, Mrs. O'Bannion.

Please, call me Grace.

If you call me Billy.

All right, Billy.

He took her hand, and his senses instantly came alive. How soft
her palm. How tapering and light her fingers.

From the caller's hollowed hands came: It's time for *Hold That
Line*. No partners on this one, so everybody on the floor. Shake a
strong hoof and join right in!

Everyone who could stand upright without a cane formed a line with arms locked behind each other's backs. As the fiddler whined his fiddlestick, the long line of dancers kicked their legs up and down like a giant centipede. Sandwiched between Billy and Grace was an enormous man possessed of a stunning lack of rhythm. Beat after beat he missed, throwing Grace hilariously off her step. Laughing, she kicked her magnificent legs even higher.

Ten minutes later came *The Gentleman's For*—the portion of the evening reserved for the gentlemen to show off their fancy footwork. The caller twanged out the steps in his metered monotone, and Billy was the first gent to lead out.

> *First gent lead out to the right of the ring,*
> *And bow real low to that pretty little thing.*
> *Now wheel around on heel and toe,*
> *Then swing around that pretty little doe.*

Billy was clicking his heels on the floor and swinging Rosa around on the dance floor, and you would never have guessed at his leg injury. Warm-faced and panting a little, Billy bowed to Rosa and jigged around by himself with his hands held over his head. Grace, acting out her part of the ritual, was barely observing him and whenever he caught her eye, looked away. In the middle of Billy's dance an absurdly tall man high-stepped over with a glass of water, crouched down and following an old Western tradition, flicked water on Billy's feet. Turning to the crowd, he shouted in a high tenor voice: His feet is on fire!

The crowd roared. The caller gave Billy, still dancing, further directions.

Now move along with another whirl,
And bow to the lady with the cute spit curl.
Now jig around on heel and toe,
Then swing her high and swing her low.
Now visit with the lady on the left,
And bow real low, so nice and deft.
Strut your stuff, boy, jig and whirl,
Then twirl around that last little girl.

Billy took the arm of Grace—the last little girl—and created a circle for her to follow, and for the first time she showed emotion in her face, and abandoning all pretense, threw her head back with delight. In this brief moment of victory, Billy was all in a glow. Other men were on the floor now, and as Billy continued his rooster strut, an elbow jabbed his back. Turning around, he discovered a gaunt gent with bony elbows, one of which was hooked onto Rosa's arm. Rosa gave Billy a look of distress as if she might never return, and the next moment was whirled away in convulsions of laughter.

Following this dance, in the center of the room, a cowboy from the Hopkins-Bingham ranch gave a display of rope twirling. From one hand came a streaming doorway that grazed the floor and ceiling, and from the other hand came a second streaming doorway. By crisscrossing his arms, the cowboy glided the doorways back and forth in a blurring vision of rope and speed, and as he jumped in and out of each gliding doorway, there was not one cowboy, but two, and the doorways had their own fluid existence independent of his smooth turning hands.

Duck for the Oyster found Grace and Billy talking next to the *Good* bowl, which was still half full, in contrast to the *Bad* bowl, which had been drained to a cat-lick puddle. Under discussion between Grace and Billy was Clark's Magnetic Mineral Waters, the natural hot springs that the Clark boy had turned into a bathing facility some twenty years ago. Billy was arguing that the waters were magnetic because of their high iron content. Grace held that the waters were magnetic because they were so alluring. She had turned away to adjust a black hair-bow on one of the bouncing Heinz twins when the two spitters approached Billy. The gun dealer spat out a question: Want to know—you think this Mason dance—the best?

Without waiting for Billy's response, the bricklayer spat out his own question: Want to know—Mason dance last month—better?

Grace interposed her body between the men and looked at Billy with wild eyes. This is a Mason dance?

Well, you see.

Grace hurried toward the door.

Grace!

But the legs that had performed so splendidly on the dance floor failed Billy when it came to covering distance rapidly. The most he could manage was a swift jerky walk. By the time he was halfway to the door, Grace had left the building.

NINETEEN

B illy called out to Grace through the passenger window of his car, and her stiff carriage conveyed her response. A second time he called out her name, and this time she permitted him a sideways glance.

I would have told you it was a Mason dance, Billy said. But you turned me down, remember?

It's late, Grace said. Moving toward the passenger door: I shouldn't walk home in the dark.

Billy reached across the seat and opened the door. Grace thanked him as she climbed inside. As Billy steered the car toward the Congress Hotel, Grace stared out the passenger window.

One thing about your husband, Billy said.

Grace turned and looked at him keenly. What about my husband?

A lot of those people at the dance tonight, they liked him. He wouldn't have been elected sheriff without their vote. And as I recall, he was up against a Mason at the time.

His opponent was a Mason?

Yes, ma'am. And no ordinary Mason at that. A thirty-third-degree Mason.

Well, those Masons aren't the worse dancers I've seen, Grace said.

Well, you don't exactly have a wooden leg yourself, Billy said.

Grace smiled a conciliatory smile, and Billy's spirit lifted. Three blocks away from the Congress, Grace turned to Billy and said she'd like to see the slag if that was all right with him. She pointed to a dark alleyway on the right and said it was a shortcut.

Billy made the turn. Poking his way down the alleyway, he came upon a group of moving shadows, men who turned their faces away from the car's headlights. The men were removing articles of used clothing from the support braces of telephone poles. The townsfolk had placed the clothing there so the men could collect it at night without showing their faces. Billy thought he could identify with the men in a way. Despite being intensely attracted to Grace, he had not shown her his true face.

Back on main street, Billy followed Grace's directions again, and this time they rolled past all the respectable buildings in town, until the road curved and threw off its paved overcoat and relaxed into the same informal dirt trail it had been for ninety years. With each bump the car complained anew, and Billy was regretting not buying the optional shock absorbers, front and rear, that the dealer had tried to sell him five years ago.

They passed the chained front gates of Walter's Brewery, a building that had not fallen into desuetude, but was simply marking time. Not that the residents of Pueblo felt any great loss at the brewery's closure. Martin Walter had learned the brewery trade at Miller in Milwaukee, but beer in Pueblo tasted nothing at all like beer in Milwaukee. And that was owing to Milwaukee water, which was clear and flowing, as opposed to Pueblo water, which stagnated in ditches, or at least that's what the tourists from Colorado Springs always said.

The car crunched its way past Bullen's Sand & Gravel, which despite its name had more dust than either sand or gravel. From Bullen's, they traversed a bridge that passed over the Arkansas, and once on the other side Billy idled the car and pointed past a stand of cedar to a shadowy butte in the distance.

That's where Coronado turned back after he abandoned his search for the Seven Golden Cities of Cibola. He left the Rio Grande in 1540 with fourteen hundred men, including slaves. A year later thirty men were all that were left.

That's a good story, Billy, Grace said, except Coronado turned back in Nebraska.

That's what the Nebraskans will tell you, Billy said, but when I was practicing the dentist trade, two of my patients were Utes. And both men told me their ancestors were Coronado's guides and that Coronado turned back at that very butte.

Grace gave him a look that was edging toward disbelief, but it was dark in the car, and Billy didn't pick up on the shading of her expression. He put the car into low gear, and they followed the dirt road up the hill to the steel mill. A group of tired-looking men, hoping for an opening in the night shift, loitered by the gate. Billy passed them and continued toward the slag operation further down the road. A dozen or so cars were waiting for the fiery slag to appear, and the occupants of the cars, teenagers mostly, were steaming the windows of their cars with their own rising fire.

Grace pointed to a parking place away from the others, and Billy wheeled the car over and set the handbrake.

Patrick and I came here the first week after we moved from Denver.

To watch the slag?

We were already married, so, yes, to watch the slag.

How did you meet him?

Grace paused, and her memory kindled a warm reflection. We were introduced by a mutual friend, a prospector. I liked that Patrick was tall. And I liked that he had blue eyes. They were like your eyes. Almost translucent.

Her gaze floated into his, and Billy held it until she looked away.

Billy, it seems we're to get better acquainted, so I'm goin to tell you a secret. My past, well, no one in this town knows about it. I trained for the ballet and performed once in Denver when I was fifteen, a small part.

I heard that from Rosa.

That's not the past I'm referring to. When I was growin up, my father made a comfortable livin in Denver as a hatter, but he got bitten by the gold bug and died as a prospector in Cripple Creek. Mother and I moved to Leadville, where she got a job managing a hotel, and there she met a man who sold insurance, and they went East. I was seventeen, and I had to make a livin. And so I became a dance hall girl.

Billy tried to conceal his surprise but failed.

I know, you're thinkin I don't seem the type. Well, none of us girls was the type. We just needed to make money. Don't get me wrong, we were respectable girls. We never joined the scarlet sisterhood.

I've been to a few hurdy gurdy houses and dance halls in my day. I remember the sayin: A skirt is a skirt and must be respected as such.

Well, they respected us all right, Grace said and laughed. It was more akin to bein worshiped. You know what they used to say.

Gals in those days didn't show much of their fetlocks. And there were so few girls in Leadville back then that men would come from miles around just to glimpse our fetlocks and hear the rustle of our petticoats.

What kind of dances did you do?

Oh, everything. The do-si-do, the schottische, the cross-eyed snap. I've danced on top of a grand piano, on the counter of a bar. Once the prospectors got together in the middle of the room and made a dance floor of their hunched-over backs, and we kicked off our shoes and danced the fandango right on top of em. One of those prospectors was Patrick. I remember one night he leaned over the balcony and showered my hair with gold dust. Well, you would think my hair would have glittered with all that dust, but the gold wasn't processed so my hair didn't glitter at all. It was just like havin thick Colorado dust in your hair. But I didn't mind. I washed out my hair that night and collected ten dollars in gold.

Outside the car there was a screech of metal upon metal.

Oh, it's happenin, Grace said excitedly.

A small engine emerged from the mill, hauling four gondola cars that screeched along a track. The gondola cars were like giant teacups, and inside them sloshed the glowing slag. The small engine came to an abrupt halt, and one by one the gondola cars tipped over. Flaming rivers of molten metal came pouring out, each orange river flowing at a different speed and sending out a shower of sparks into the night.

As the rivers slowed in their descent, Grace turned her head toward Billy. I've told you about my life. Now it's your turn. Who are you, Billy? Who are you really?

Billy paused uncomfortably. Well, I was born in the Five Points area of Lower Manhattan.

From Grace's widening eyes Billy knew her curiosity was blooming.

A New York City boy. That's a good start. What were you like as a boy?

I was a reader, a big reader.

Mark Twain?

The Police Gazette.

Oh, literature.

Billy gained confidence from her smile. When I was ten, my family moved to the territory of New Mexico. Don't remember much about it, except for the time I took a pair of pants from a clothesline.

You didn't have your own pants?

I wanted to imitate somethin I had read.

So you like to pretend.

Well, in some ways I suppose I do. But I returned the pants to the clothesline the next day, which, in some ways, was even more excitin.

He hesitated as new images took form in his mind. All in all, I was a good kid who just had some bad breaks.

Bad breaks?

At one point I was charged with stealin some blankets from a Chinese laundry, but it was my friend Sombrero Jack who stole em, stashed em in my room and hightailed it out of town to let me take the rap. The sheriff knew I was innocent, but he put me in jail anyway. I think he just wanted to scare me. He was real friendly like, and on the second day of my imprisonment he let me swing my arms in the hallway to get some exercise. And findin myself alone, I took the opportunity to crawl up the chimney, leavin behind a few grains of soot to indicate how I made my escape.

Billy broke off his reminiscence and his mind waited on her re-action, but as she had none, he continued, his eyes shining. Well, after that experience, I wanted to be a real outlaw, so I joined up with the Jesse Evans gang and lifted horses. The Lincoln County War came along, and that's when I got shot in my leg. After the war was over, I returned to horse-liftin and, well, I remember one time when two officers were in a saloon. They tried to protect their horses with long picket ropes that stretched into the bar. Well, I just cut the ropes, tied em to the railing and lifted their horses.

Billy glanced over at his passenger. Grace's upper body had tensed emphatically, and Billy could see in the glow of the orange light that her eyes were grading him.

Take me home, Grace said as the light subsided. I tell you some-thin nobody else in this town knows, and you—you give me a rehash of the book you're writin.

Caught unprepared, Billy opened his mouth and waited for some mollifying words to roll forth, but no sound came to his lips. Panic seized upon him. Escape, if any, would come through a dar-ing counterplay. After a lengthy pause, he whispered: Grace, I'm not who I said I was.

Grace's breathing deepened. Then who are you? She was sitting straight, chin lifted, listening. Her frank eyes would accept nothing but the truth.

I'm a retired dentist from New York City. I've led a very dull life, and I beg your indulgence. And with this greatest of admis-sions Billy fell silent.

Grace blushed for him. There now. Don't you feel better?

He did not. But all he could find to answer was yes, he did feel better. He gazed at Grace's face, lit by the slag. The afterglow made a nimbus of her hair and briefly gave her the appearance of a saint. Sinners and their saints, he said to himself. He wanted to gather her in his arms and bend his face closer to hers, but she was watching the last glowing bits of metal roll down the embankment like giant orange tears, and when he looked closer, he could see her face had taken on a reflective cast, and he knew she was inhabiting some distant memory.

I enjoyed myself tonight, Grace said, interrupting her own thoughts and glancing back at him. And now I'm ready to go home.

Billy took the car back to the hotel and parked it. He climbed out, circled around to the passenger side and opened the door. Grace took his hand as she brought her feet to the pavement and released his hand as she stood up. The night was dark and windless, and they walked toward the hotel in the darkness without conversation. In silence they entered the hotel and in silence they walked up the stairs. Then they were standing before Grace's hotel room, and Grace had her body turned away from him. Her right hand inserted the key while her left hand gripped the doorknob. She turned her head and thanked him for a most interesting night and said wasn't that slag something to see, and Billy said it was, and Grace opened the door and said goodnight, and Billy said goodnight, and he waited until she had clicked the door shut before turning around and walking down the hallway to his room.

TWENTY

A t his writing desk later that night Billy underlined his favorite passages in *Billy the Kid: Outlaw or Hero*. He was nearing the end of the book on this latest reading when he heard gunshots outside. He tossed a glance through the blinds. Plato was leaning beside the unpainted door and drunkenly firing his pistol at a street sign at the far end of the street, making a different pinging sound with each bullet. The effect was almost musical. Abruptly the door opened, and Stokes emerged, half in shadow, half in light. He spoke to Plato in a low voice, and Plato nodded and moved toward the entrance, and pointing his pistol at the night sky, fired a last round at the stars.

Billy raised his eyes to the stars. The stars and the constellations were off course tonight. His mind turned to the beautiful swarming stars of his youth, the stars that guided the Kid in the Chihuahuan Desert after his horse and boots were stolen. The stars that had been his boon companions. The stars that had fled reluctantly with the desert dawn, leaving the Kid to wander on the hot sands in his stocking feet under a massacring sun. The Mescalero who found him lying on the ground was riding a pony painted with the sacred symbols. He tipped water down the Kid's throat from a dried gourd and applied a poultice to the Kid's chapped and swollen feet, naming each plant he was using. In this way the Kid learned *astaneh* was the mescal plant, and *huskane* the yucca plant, and *nastaneh* the mesquite plant. The Kid observed that the medicine man was old and had bunches of nettles lashed to his legs, and he supposed they were there to increase circulation. As the healing ceremony began, the Mescalero chanted the sacred medicine song over the Kid's body, and with the chanting the Kid became calm, and a peace like a cool afternoon breeze swept over him. He closed his eyes, and instantly an energy began moving inside him like a living thing. The energy circulated from his head to his toes, and from his toes to his head again. Gathering in a concentrated point at the crown of his head, the energy pierced through his skull and became a hovering energy over his body. And all at once the Kid discovered he was the hovering energy itself, observing the ministrations of the Mescalero as the Mescalero chanted the medicine song and shook the coyote medicine rattle in interlocking circles. Two sharp shakes, the rattling stopped, and the next moment the Kid found himself in a landscape altogether different.

He struggled to get his new bearings. And in a rush, it came to him. He was inside a large barn where a baile was taking place, and huddled together against the wall were three of his muchachas. Back and forth, in time to the music, they swayed their dresses. One of the muchachas was Paulita Maxwell, his undisputed favorite. He had first seen her at a baile a week ago, and he had tracked her through the barn like a rooster treading a hen, and when she was alone he had caught her arm and spoken to her, much to the displeasure of her brother, Pete, who had observed their interaction from across the barn. But Paulita was her own woman and

always had the jaunty air of impudence about her, and in allowing
the Kid to speak to her—a white man wanted by the law—she
had cheerfully flouted the restrictions of her race and sex. The
Kid knew she had a lot of suitors, but he had sworn to himself
he would have the first dance with her. And although he was the
dancer to whom all hearts were given, it was Paulita he wanted,
Paulita of the quick laughter and the lithe figure, Paulita of the
falling dark curls and flashing dark eyes, Paulita—he would have
her. Glancing at his reflection in the back of his pocket watch, he
observed with approval how his sandy blond hair splashed onto
his shoulders. An hour earlier he had scented his hair with cinna-
mon after the manner of George Armstrong Custer, though there
was nothing about Custer he liked, except for the way he wore his
hair. And because Paulita favored men who turned themselves out
for a baile, he had spent a month's salary on a pair of waxed Jeff
Davis brogans, a ready-made shirt and trousers, and now, here he
was, looking like some fresh-faced country jake with the barrel
and cylinder of his Colt jammed in the front waistband of his pants
because he didn't want to ruin his slick by strapping on a worn-
out holster. Wearing shoes instead of boots for the first time in his
life, he was feeling like an imposter, but he didn't care a whit, not
a whit. Tonight he was going to dance with his favorite muchacha.
And before the stroke of midnight he would dance her right out of
the barn, and she would be his querida. With this promise to himself he blinked his eyes, and instantly he was dancing with Paulita
on the plank wood flooring, and he was making her laugh with
his ridiculously good footwork, and as the song slowed, his steps
slowed, and he was whispering to her in all the fullness of his heart
that he would make her his wife someday, and she was lowering

her long dark eyelashes in embarrassment, and he was thinking he had frightened her with his boldness, but when she raised her face the next moment she bore so wide a smile that he was unable to contain himself and kissed her right there on the dance floor and kept kissing her and kissing her until her brother Pete tapped him twice on the shoulder.

Twice the coyote medicine rattle shook inside the Kid's head, and now the rhythmic chanting of the medicine song transported him from the baile to another place and time, and suddenly he was sitting astride a bay mare next to a field of foot-high bunchgrass, and Paulita was leaning her forearm against his saddle, tracing with her forefinger the design he had carved with a swivel knife. It was his first meeting with her outside of the baile, and he was desperate to impress her. Reaching over, he crossed her palm with two silver dollars and instructed her to throw the coins high in the air when he was about thirty yards away, and Paulita nodded her head vigorously and said: *Sí, entiendo.* When he was certain she had understood the instructions, he trotted the mare to a copse of oak trees, turned around and halted like a stadium bull waiting for the right moment to charge. He tapped his boot heels on the mare's flanks and with a yip, yip, yip, he was galloping toward her, twirling his two Colts in opposite directions. Paulita raised her closed fist up and down in the air, as if to prime the pump of her heart for the thrilling adventure that would be her new life with him, the mare thundering toward her, fifty, forty, thirty yards away, and high into the air she threw the contents of her hand, which were not the two coins, however, but a handful of loose bunch-grass, and she tossed her head back laughing, her dark hair cascading over her shoulders. Reining in his horse beside her, the Kid broke into high-pitched laughter, wiping his face with his hand. He wheeled around his horse, shouting for her to do it right this time, or else, and back to the starting point he went. He breathed, the horse breathed and he was ready. Again his wild charge. Again his twirling guns. Again Paulita raising and lowering her fist. At last, into the air, she released silver, but only a single coin, a coin that nonetheless the Kid shot dead in the center, spinning it in the air like some shiny spinning mechanical insect before it fell to the earth with the weight of its own impossibility. Almost as an afterthought Paulita tossed the other silver dollar over her shoulder into the bunchgrass, and the Kid raced his horse toward her in such a fury that Paulita screamed to high heaven and fled into the bunchgrass, and he chased her with his mare, cutting a serpentine swath and springing off his mount and tackling her onto the bunchgrass, and bouncing his elbow off a hidden rock, and yelping with the pain, and Paulita covering her mouth to smother her amusement. With his one good arm the Kid grabbed her and embraced her, and they rolled around in the bunchgrass, laughing and kissing, and Paulita kissing his elbow with rapid tiny kisses, and the Kid rolling on top of her and pressing his weight against her, and Paulita devouring him with searing kisses, and her breath coming hot and fast, and sweet sounds escaping her mouth, and the Kid's name repeated over and over again. The Kid closed his eyes in carnal bliss, until two sharp shakes of the medicine rattle assailed his ear. Once more he could hear the chanting of the medicine song, and when he opened his eyes, he found himself in the early evening light, and no longer lying in the bunchgrass, but standing upright in a different place altogether.

He was in an orchard. A peach orchard. It was an orchard he knew well. The orchard bordered the white picket fence that marked out the property of the big adobe house where Paulita lived. On many an evening he had blotted himself against a tree while waiting for her brother, Pete, to leave the property, but something inside him told him there was one occupant in the house now, and he knew who it was. The sky darkened, and he found himself directing his gaze at a glowing light in a window, the window going dark and another window glowing and the second window going dark. He heard the front door opening, and Paulita appeared on the verandah with a glowing lantern that was spilling a river of gold over the floorboards, her long hair escaping her bonnet in dark waves and her skin lit to a golden hue. She was searching the darkness for someone, but there was no one around except the Kid, and she couldn't see him. He tried to call out to her but could not. He tried to move toward her but could not. He was not inhabiting his body this time, but existing in his spirit, and he was there not to participate, but to observe. Paulita turned toward the door, the golden light streaming behind her on the verandah, and it was then he observed a streak of gray in her hair he had never seen before. Before he could contemplate what this meant, Paulita swung the lantern back inside the house and disappeared.

With the shutting of the door, the Kid's eyes closed shut, and when they opened he was standing outside Paulita's bedroom, peering in through the window. Paulita was by her dresser, a tintype photograph clutched in her hand. The face on the photograph—it was his face. He had given the photograph to her on her eighteenth birthday, and here she was with a gray streak in her hair gazing at his photograph with unabashed affection. He wanted to be in the room with her, to reach out to her, to caress her check, but no sooner did he have this thought than he heard the crunching of boots in the house, and from the other room a stranger's voice called out her name. Paulita wiped her eyes with the tips of her forefingers, and there was a new expression on her face, an expression of peace, if not of contentment, and she slipped the photograph under the mattress of the iron-framed bed and came forth from the room with the glowing lantern, and through the crack of the door the Kid observed her embracing a man in the shadows, a man he had never seen before, but a man he knew was her future husband. Observing this scene of betrayal, he could feel a sinking in his heart, but he also felt curiously relieved, knowing part of Paulita still loved him, and if for any reason he was absent from her life in the future, she would not court loneliness, but would choose the braver path—to love another.

Two shakes of the rattle, and the chanting of the medicine song ended, and next thing the Kid knew he was back in his body, and he was fluttering his eyes under the desert sun, his body stronger than before, but still too weak to walk, to even ride, and next to him, the Mescalero was speaking softly to the pony that was painted with the sacred symbols, and the Mescalero making a simple hand gesture, and the pony, understanding both word and gesture, lying down on the ground, and the Mescalero helping the Kid climb onto the pony's bare back, and the Mescalero speaking softly to the pony again and making a different hand gesture this time, and the pony standing up, and the Mescalero swinging up his body forward of the Kid, between the pony's shoulder and barrel, and in this manner they rode for five hours, with a low withers the pony was easy to ride this way, the Kid chewing black seeds for energy from the Mescalero's deerskin pouch and pointing out the way until they reached the white picket fence of Paulita's ranch house, and the Mescalero dismounting, the pony sitting down at his word and gesture, and the Kid dismounting, and the Mescalero helping him along to the gate, and bursting from the front door of the ranch house came Paulita, garbed in her washing clothes, a high warm color in her cheeks, her hair up in a bun, stray curls curling out, and saying Billy Billy Billy with tears coursing down her cheeks, and wrapping her arms around him and gently kissing his burnt face, and the Kid rejoicing, knowing his future dream had not yet come to pass, and Paulita and the Mescalero half-walking, half-carrying him up to the front porch and into the house and into her bedroom and laying him down on the iron-framed bed, and Billy looking at the Mescalero and thanking him saying *ah-heh-heh-eh*, and the Mescalero saying *ash* and turning around and walking out of the house in moccasined feet that never made a sound and mounting the pony with the sacred symbols to ride back to the land of his people.

TWENTY-ONE

The next day as Billy was coming down the staircase of the hotel, Tommy sprang up the stairs to accost him.

Said you were goin to tell me. Proudly he showed his schoolbooks. School is over for the day in case you were wonderin.

Tell you what, Tommy?

What it's like to kill a man.

Reaching the floor, Billy said in a quiet voice: You pull the trigger. That's all there is to it. He fired an imaginary pistol to show the simplicity of it.

How many of the men you killed were good men, like the deputy? Tommy said, dogging Billy's heels as Billy strode out of the hotel.

A few of em, Billy said.

Then why did you kill em?

Afternoon, Billy, said a female voice.

Billy tapped the brim of his hat. Afternoon, Grace.

He sauntered down the sidewalk, waiting until she was out of earshot and spoke to Tommy again. Like I told you, I killed the first man in a barroom brawl, defendin myself. But I got a taste for it, you might say. And after that I would shoot any man if there was a reason to do so.

So you got a taste for it? You mean it felt good when you killed a man?

Yeah, it felt good.

Even the good men you killed? It felt good to kill em?

Every time it felt good, no matter if the man was bad or good.

So why did you stop your killin?

I didn't like that feelin.

But you just told me it felt good.

It did feel good. But I didn't like the feelin, just the same.

So how'd you stop? You told me before it wasn't love, it wasn't marriage.

Billy paused beside the door to his car and looked at Tommy thoughtfully. It's about the light and the power of the light.

The light?

You know about Dracula?

Everyone knows about Dracula.

And when sunlight falls on Dracula's body, what happens?

He dies.

That's right, Tommy, he dies. So it's like this. You take the darkness outside of you, all of it, every last bit, and lay it all out in the blazin light. Don't let none of it fall into shadow, just lay it all out in the blazin light, makin sure every part of it is shot through with the light, and just look at it deeply and completely, and if you do that, if you really do that.

Tommy looked at him, listening, expectant. And if you do that, then what?

If you do that, the darkness dies. The darkness that was livin inside you dies. It just dies. And then it is no more.

So that's what happened to your feelin?

That's what happened. I threw light all over that dark feelin, every last part of it, and that dark feelin just died.

Did it ever come back, that dark feelin?

Never. It never came back. Not the littlest bit. Nothin.

Where you goin? Tommy said as Billy climbed into his car.

Time for the Spit 'n' Argue.

～

Five blocks away from the Thatcher building, where the Spit 'n' Argue meeting was to take place, Billy slackened his car to a crawl. Embedded in the trunk of a sycamore tree was the fine mesh grille of a brand-new Cadillac Coupe. Plato was slouched against the trunk of the tree, his eyes glassy and unblinking. From his hand dangled a bottle of hooch. Billy trickled the wheels of his car closer. He called out the window: Need a lift?

The voice shattered Plato's reverie, and the bottle in his hand smashed to the ground. With despair he stared at the spreading liquid and drank with his eyes what his throat would never savor. Lifting his head, he beheld the man who had disturbed his meditation. He was about to say something when he got caught in a sudden gale of insobriety and blew sideways, first in one direction and another, eventually gusting over to Billy's car. As if to ascertain the reality of the vehicle, he ran his hand along the front fender, up the edge of the windshield and along the roof until he smacked a spot above the driver's open window. Thrusting his blue chin inside the car, he said in a gruff voice: What you want?

Get in. I'll take you to Wally's garage. He'll tow your car, fix it up.

Plato stared at him, withdrew his face and spun around. Six exaggerated steps took him back to his Cadillac. He paused as if to consider what to do next and abruptly threw his torso inside the open window. With a grievous effort he pulled himself out again, and in his hand there now dangled a pistol. Into his waistband he stuffed the pistol and began an obstacle course of his own making, jumping over a rock, slamming his boot down on a rattlesnake hole and at one point balancing—for an instant only—on one foot like a stork. Eventually arriving back at Billy's car, he felt his way over to the passenger door, wrested it open and threw himself inside.

As Billy steered the car into the street, he glanced at the protruding handle of Plato's pistol. A Remington Single-Action, he said. Haven't seen one of those in years.

I was shootin at some crows, Plato said absently.

While you were drivin?

Ain't no fun if I'm stationary. I'm a philosopher, you know.

So I heard. And what do you philosophize about?

Death.

Death. And what's your view on death?

That it don't exist, not at all.

How do you figure?

You believe in the human spirit? Plato said, his eyes glinting.

The human spirit?

I believe the human spirit is immortal. So that makes death an illusion.

Billy glanced at the Remington. How many men you killed?

How can I kill anyone if death don't exist? Plato said with a grin.

What do you call it when you fire your gun at a man?

I shoot the blindin light of eternity into the shadows of humanity.

How many men, how many shadows you light up like that?

Eighteen.

How does it feel?

Feel? Plato gave him a blank stare.

Yeah, when you light a man up like that, how does it feel?

Don't feel like nothin. The voice of the man contained not a single particle of emotion.

Billy rolled the Model T up the apron of Wally's Auto-Repair Shop. He turned to Plato. That's Wally workin under the car, he said, pointing to a pair of legs underneath a Pontiac in the service bay. He's got a tow truck for you.

Wally, Plato said under his breath. By degrees he extricated himself from Billy's car. Holding on to the passenger door for support, he appraised the repair shop as if plotting his next move.

One thing, Billy said.

Plato cranked his head around with annoyance.

Peck and his boys will blow your head off if they see you.

Plato's grin returned. What they'll see is the blindin light of eternity.

A shove of his hand propelled him several yards. Lunging for the side of the garage, he caught the edge of the open door and swung himself inside. Gravity pulled him to the floor, and there he sat, legs splayed, waiting for Wally to slide out from underneath the car.

TWENTY-TWO

Missed the club meeting today, the gun dealer said to Billy.

You didn't miss nothin, Billy, exceptin some spit and some argue, the bricklayer said.

Speak for yourself, the gun dealer said.

Who else? the bricklayer said.

The three men were at the counter of the diner, drinking coffee. Even though the lunch hour had long passed, there were no booths to be had. It was Friday and that meant the place was full of Catholics from the southside, the section of town south of the Arkansas River. The strict edict of their faith forbade the eating of meat on Fridays, but their Catholic brethren north of the Arkansas River had received a special dispensation by the local diocese allowing them to eat whatever they wanted, so every Friday a sprinkling of southside Catholics traveled over the bridge into the freewheeling, flesh-eating northside, and there they converged on the Congress Hotel or Earl's Diner, and at the Congress they ate porterhouse steaks, or lamb chops with mint jelly, and at Earl's Diner they ate hamburgers, or ham and eggs, and they ate amply and without guilt.

Rosa reached over from the serving side of the counter and topped off Billy's cup. Lowering her voice to a whisper, she said: *que ibas a decirme cuándo?*

Tell you what, Rosa?

Thought I was your confidante, she said.

Qué quieres saber, Rosa?

Rosa glanced at the two spitters who were arguing amongst themselves. Moving around the counter, she perched on the stool next to Billy.

You're not who you say you are.

What?

You're not Billy the Kid. You're someone, but you're not him.

Billy looked over his shoulder to see if the spitters had heard. They had not. They were arguing the merits of vintage pistols. The gun dealer was extolling the virtues of the Colt Single-Action Army pistol. The bricklayer was singing the praises of the Single-Action Smith & Wesson Russian model, a gun so reliable it became the official handgun of the Russian army in the 1880's.

I wasn't snoopin, Rosa said to Billy in the same subdued voice. Grace O'Bannion was in the booth, writin in her diary, and the page was open. People don't realize I can read upside-down as easily as right-side up.

Well, it's not true.

I know it's not true. I just think you could have told me first.

I mean it's not true what Grace wrote in her diary. And I'm goin to tell her so.

He stood up. Rosa stood up beside him, and he clutched her wrist. His voice was low and insistent. Grace O'Bannion is wrong.

I am Billy the Kid, and when my book comes out, you'll see for yourself. Everyone will.

He glanced at the two spitters. They were deep in argument. Billy waited for a pause in their debate and then addressed them both, saying the best single-action pistol in the old days was the Merwin Hulbert. It loaded like a Colt with six individual rounds, but there was a latch in front of the trigger guard that turned the housing out ninety degrees. And only the shells you used fell out. The rest remained in place.

For the first time in their lives, the spitters were rendered silent.

Of course, as you know, I preferred a Colt Double-Action Thunderer, Billy said. The sheer stark power. No cockin the gun. Just pull the trigger.

But fire like that, muzzle moves, the gun dealer said.

Lose accuracy, Colt Double-Action Thunderer, the bricklayer said.

You can compensate, Billy said.

How? the gun dealer said.

By bein a crack shot, Billy said.

Verily, the bricklayer said.

Verily, the gun dealer said.

Billy placed his hat on his head and advanced to the door in a sharp jerky walk. Taking a deep breath, he opened the door and set forth on his woeful errand.

～

When Grace answered the knock on the door, she had a pair of men's full-cut trousers over her arm. What a coincidence, Billy, she said. I was just goin to knock on your door.

Grace, there's somethin you and I should talk about.

Come in, why don't you.

As Billy stepped inside, Grace crossed over to an armchair. Draped over the back was an assortment of men's clothing. She placed the trousers to one side and patted them affectionately. Plus Fours, she said with a faint note of hilarity. Patrick read about em in a magazine. There was an article about Edward VII and how he was wearin Plus Fours, a patterned Fair Isle sweater and a white butterfly-collared shirt. Of course, Crews-Beggs didn't stock em. So Patrick ordered all of em by mail. Naturally he never wore em. Can you imagine a sheriff in Pueblo wearin Plus Fours and a patterned Fair Isle sweater on his day off? The good citizens of this town would have thrown him in jail for impersonatin a New York playboy.

One by one, she peeled back the other garments. There was a light-colored sheriff's suit with a wide-lapel sack jacket, a dark blue three-piece suit, two blue striped ties, several white collared shirts, two pairs of Levi jeans, and a yellow sweater vest. She picked up the sweater vest and rubbed the fabric between her fingers.

It's cashmere. Patrick wore it only once.

Grace.

She held up the sweater vest by the shoulders and laid it against Billy's chest. It's your size.

Grace.

Her eyes welled up. Please, take it, just take it.

Billy took the sweater vest and slung it over his forearm, and a second later Grace was covering her face with both hands. I don't know what to do with it all. I really don't know what to do. It's been three years, and I can't seem to throw out anything, but I can't have it here anymore. I kissed him goodbye in the morning, and two hours later he was dead. I never had a chance to say goodbye, you know? To say goodbye and I love you. I'm sorry, I didn't mean to get like this. I couldn't cry at his funeral. I don't know why. Everything happened so fast, you know? And now I feel like I'm givin up the last part of him. It's tough. It's really tough. But I have to do it. I have to. I just have to.

Billy moved toward the pile of clothes. Let me take em for you.

Grace pressed her fingertips together. Oh, I'd be so abidingly grateful.

He placed the sweater vest on top of the other clothes and gathered them into his arms. I had a great love once that didn't work out, Billy said. I kept a sweater of hers for years.

What was her name?

Paulita.

Where did you meet her?

On a ranch near Fort Sumner. It was a long time ago.

Paulita—as in Paulita Maxwell?

Yes, Paulita Maxwell, Billy the Kid's girlfriend, my girlfriend.

I can't believe this, Billy. I tell you about my personal trials, and you tell me your old stories again.

Grace, I am Billy the Kid. That's what I came here to tell you.

Dr. McCarty, you can't continue this charade. The other night you told me.

What you wanted to hear.

What I wanted to hear. Well, what I want to hear right now is your footsteps as you be leavin this room.

His eyes left hers and sought the door. She opened the door and held it open, and he passed into the hallway without a glance, without a word, carrying her dead memories in his arms.

TWENTY-THREE

Toward noon the next day, Billy pushed his pencil aside, rose from his writing desk and went over to the mirror. From the top corner he removed the auction notice and folded it into his wallet. He checked his appearance lest Grace O'Bannion appear unexpectedly in the hallway. His right collar had curled up at the end. He ironed it down with his fingertips, left the room and went into the hallway. Grace was nowhere in sight.

Parking outside Peck's Place, Billy glanced around for any sign of Stokes or his men. Finding none, he climbed out of his car, mounted the steps to the saloon, pushed through the swinging doors and met the smiling face of the bartender.

The bartender, in rolled shirtsleeves, was polishing a glass. Throwing the bar towel over his shoulder: What can I get you, Billy?

How about some self-respect?

How about a beer?

How about a Coca-Cola?

How about it?

The bartender thudded the bottle on the counter and struck off the bottle cap with a hammer. Billy took a long draft, glancing over at Peck, who was speaking to a glass fitter. The glass fitter had just installed a skylight in the ceiling to afford Peck a view of the stars at night.

Peck finished with the glass fitter and crossed over to Billy. Now you're comin here when I'm not even payin you. I'll fix up a bedroom in the back so you never have to leave. To the bartender: This man here is to have whatever he wants so long as he never pays for it. If he pays for it, or even tries to pay for it, kick him out.

What if he leaves a tip? the bartender said.

You have a gun.

Shoot the man?

Shoot the tip.

Billy stretched his lips into a smile and said to Peck: Dropped by to tell you I'm goin to an auction in Denver tonight. I won't be here, but the rest of my band will.

What's at the auction?

Billy took out the auction notice from his wallet and read from it: Winchester New Model '73. Reputed to be the rifle of legend used by Billy the Kid.

What does Billy the Kid think?

Billy folded the auction notice and put it back in his wallet. If it's genuine, he'll buy it.

Found three dead crows on the road today, Peck said in a confidential tone. They weren't shot up or nothin. It was more like they just fell out of the sky. It's a sign, Billy. Somethin is goin to happen here real soon. You don't want to miss out on that.

In truth, I do want to miss out on that.

You've changed, Dr. McCarty.

That I have.

Billy took another swig of his Coca-Cola, walked out of the saloon and headed toward his car. Before reaching the driver's door, he glimpsed a shadow on his right side and spun around so quickly that the owner of the shadow stumbled backward and almost fell to the ground.

Howdy, Tommy.

No school today, Billy.

What's on your mind, Tommy?

That feeling you talked about. The feeling you liked, but didn't like, that went away with the power of the light.

What about it?

That light that replaced the darkness. Was that light the Unseen?

Billy gripped the door handle of his car. What's on your mind, Tommy?

Pa said he stopped believin in anything after Ma died of the Spanish influenza. And I stopped believin in anything too. But I got to thinkin if I start believin in the Unseen that maybe the Unseen will protect my Pa.

It doesn't work like that.

Then who's goin to look out for him?

I'll speak to your Pa again, tell him to stay away from those bad men.

The corners of Tommy's mouth drooped down. What I don't understand is why people go bad in the first place.

Why? Lots of reasons, I suppose. For one thing we don't see that anymore. Billy was pointing to a mountain peak in the distance.

I don't understand.

I'll tell you what, Tommy. If we could ever see that mountain peak, see it truly, the immensity of its beauty would pervade our souls.

And then?

And then our lives would change forever.

Change forever how?

It's different for each person.

Was there ever a time when we could see truly?

Maybe there was, but I don't know.

Billy climbed inside the car, but before he could shut the door, Tommy inserted himself in the opening.

Like the Mescaleros? Can they see truly?

Some of em can, I imagine.

Which ones?

The ones with the least civilizin.

Think we'll ever see truly again?

Maybe, if we can ever step out of the way.

Step out of the way of what?

Ourselves.

With these last words Billy started the engine, and Tommy stepped back and shut the driver's door.

Gunslinger! came a treble voice from across the street. Billy glanced over. The young cowboy had a pistol trained on the car. Billy stuck his hand out the driver's window, and with his thumb and forefinger shot the young cowboy in the gut. Twice the young cowboy twirled around before dropping dead at his mother's feet. His mother waved to Billy, and Billy blew smoke off the tip of his forefinger and sped the car down the street.

TWENTY-FOUR

A Model T built before 1926 was constructed of light steel sheets over a wood frame, and the car could reach more than 30 miles per hour on a good road. By contrast, Billy's 1927 model was constructed of heavy steel, no wood, and weighed over 1500 pounds, and he was lucky if he could get 25 miles per hour with a good wind behind him. With no speedometer it was all guesswork, anyway.

The flat empty road stretching before Billy was an extension of the Santa Fe Trail. The road bisected a desert of scrubland, and the first geographical feature of note was a piñon tree that took forty minutes to reach, one second to pass and another to forget.

With each ripple on the road Billy could feel his bones jar, and it made him think he really had gone soft, after all. He remembered meeting an ex-government agent from Camp Robinson where Crazy Horse had spent his last days. The agent told him that when Crazy Horse was mortally wounded in a scuffle, the great warrior had refused to be placed on a bed and instead insisted on spending his last few hours lying on the ground, saying the earth was his relation. Billy thought he understood the great warrior's thinking. As a young man in New Mexico Territory, he was enamored of living under the open sky. He loved slaking his thirst from a mountain stream and listening to campfire sticks cracking beneath an iron pot and breathing smoke from a wood fire. He was a cherisher of horses, cattle, birds and trees. He couldn't predict the future by observing the flight of birds the way a Mescalero medicine man could, but he had studied the habits of birds for hours on end. He liked to watch the nuthatches as they marched down the trees head-first, showing every other bird what was possible. And the hummingbirds—he liked how they suspended themselves in mid-air, and how they darted forwards and backwards in the blink of an eye. Some of his gunfighter moves came from the hummingbird, he used to say. But if he had to pick out a single bird as his totem, a bird to love and to protect, it would be the starling, not for its beauty, of which it had none, but for its song, which could mimic the lilt and tone of any Apache dialect. But mostly he liked the starling because it was the true vagabond of the bird nation, it loved the open country, and when a group of them congregated in great murmurations, rising and falling and singing and chattering and carving up the air with their swooping grandeur, no creature of the air could hope to compare.

Twenty minutes past the piñon tree, there appeared the ghostly edifice of the Standard Oil refinery. Built by Rockefeller sixteen years earlier, the once-vaunted edifice was now a rookery for desert scrub birds. But the structure still clung to the mad dream it would someday be rescued, so it whistled hopefully, forlornly, to every vehicle that passed by.

Onward moved Billy's car, and by and by a series of red panels came into view.

DOES YOUR HUSBAND

MISBEHAVE

GRUNT AND GRUMBLE

RANT AND RAVE

BUY THE BRUTE

SOME BURMA-SHAVE

Another hour along the road, and the air thickened with haze from the sun, and stray beams of light dazzled Billy's eyes. Billy found himself blinking, but not because of the light. He was blinking because he could not believe what he was looking at. Some five hundred yards in the distance a church had taken up residence in the middle of the road. A church with a steeple and cottonwood trees on either side of the entrance. The church and the trees were shimmering and made beautiful by the reflected light. As Billy's car moved ahead on the road, the church and the trees moved ahead also. No matter how fast nor how slow his car moved, the church and the trees remained exactly the same distance ahead. Billy blinked his eyes once more. A man—no, two men—were now standing among the trees. The church, the trees and the men continued to travel ahead on the road for the next little while, until the men disappeared as if claimed by another world. The church and the trees lasted a few seconds more and melted away in the rays of the sun.

An hour of oppressive heat followed. Gradually the air cooled, a slight breeze picked up, and two tumbleweeds spun toward the car, challenging it to a race. Overtaking the car, the tumbleweeds crisscrossed the road twenty yards ahead to mock with their speed and agility the mechanical conveyances of man. And once they had demonstrated their superiority in this manner, they cheerfully spun away, never to be seen again. A short time later Billy parked by the side of the road and got out of the car. Tied to the back bumper was a Minnequa Flax Car Water Bag. He untied the water bag from the bumper and tipped the metal spout to his lips. The wind from the drive had cooled the water inside, and Billy drank small cool sips under the late afternoon sun.

A sudden flash of yellow wings, and Billy glanced up. It was a meadowlark, darting above his head and moving in buoyant bumps along a swift current of air. Billy listened to the bursts of sweet fluted song, his hand clutching the water bag, and he kept listening as the meadowlark's song becoming fainter and fainter until only the soft buzzing of insects remained.

An hour outside of Denver, the sky unfurled lilac pennants across the horizon. Joining in the celebration, the sun threw a cape of shimmering gold over the scrubland, and even the green yucca plants had a golden luster on their leaf-swords, their bell-shaped flowers now gold-kissed fairy bells. There were thin streaks of gold on the hood of the car, and Billy's thoughts turned inward, and he began thinking of the gold that had dusted Grace's head that night in Leadville, and how motes of gold must have kissed her forehead, her cheeks, her lips.

By degrees, Grace's image faded from his mind, and Billy's thoughts grew slower and slower still until his mind was emptied of every image and every thought and every word. As the car rolled on, a vast stillness filled the landscape. The stillness filled the car. The stillness filled Billy and thrummed deep inside him. This sublime feeling, which was a state of being, continued until Billy entered Denver.

~

Toward eight o'clock that evening Billy entered a large room teeming with buyers. He signed his name on a sheet of paper, received a bidding paddle and took a seat in the middle of the room. Next to him sat a rancher, from Carson City, Nevada, with eyes ablaze. The rancher said he had come to buy a ghost shirt once worn by the Indian prophet Wovoka. Billy asked what he planned to do with the shirt once he bought it, and the rancher said in a flat tone he would burn it. Billy asked the rancher what he had against ghost shirts, and the rancher fixed his eyes on him and said the shirt was of pagan origin, and therefore to be destroyed. Billy asked if there was anything in the Bible that specifically mentioned the burning of ghost shirts, and the rancher allowed there was not, but said God had anointed him as his soldier in a tent revival meeting two weeks ago, and he knew now what war he must wage.

The first lot for sale was a peace-pipe that once belonged to Sitting Bull. The auctioneer began by pointing out the notches close to the mouthpiece and describing how the stem was studded with brass tacks and carved with spiral ridges. The bowl, he pointed out, was hand-rubbed and made of pipeclay.

The bidding began at ten dollars, and it climbed in increments of two dollars until the hammer fell at eighty-six dollars. It would have gone a lot higher, Billy thought, if Sitting Bull had not sold a dozen similar pipes at Buffalo Bill's Wild West Show. Next up was a brown Stetson with a pink ribbon trim, a hat once worn by Annie Oakley. The item came with an accompanying photograph of Annie wearing the hat next to Buffalo Bill, who reportedly had presented it to her. The bidding was brisk, and the hat fetched more than three times the amount of the pipe.

The auctioneer announced the third lot. A young female assistant brought out the Winchester, removed its dust cover and held the rifle high in the air to stir the crowd. But she need not have done so. The audience was rapt with attention.

Here we have a Winchester New Model of 1873, the auctioneer said. It's also known as The Gun that Won the West. It has a stock and forearm of burled walnut. It's a lever-action rifle and carries a dozen center-fired cartridges, with each .44 caliber bullet ignited by 40 grains of black powder. It was the favored rifle of Buffalo Bill and Chapa, the son of Geronimo. But this here particular gun is reputed to have belonged to Billy the Kid, the fastest gun in the West. Bidding opens at $200.

In two minutes the bidding, leaping twenty-five dollars at a time, hit $800. Goin once, goin twice, the auctioneer said, and Billy raised his paddle.

The auctioneer clocked Billy's bid at $825 and called for a counterbid. There was none. The auctioneer asked Billy to raise his paddle for the number, but instead Billy rose to his feet, turning his paddle inward at his leg.

Check first to see if there are any initials inscribed on the barrel, Billy said.

A murmur went through the crowd.

If the initials W.B. aren't on the underside of the barrel, Billy said, the gun is a fake.

The female assistant handed the rifle to the auctioneer who glanced at the underside of the barrel. Lowering the rifle, he gave Billy a look of surprise. The initials are there, he said. How'd ye know, sir?

On account of the fact I'm William Bonney, otherwise known as Billy the Kid.

At once the room was awash with whispers. Billy nodded his head to the left and the right and smiled at the perplexed faces. Turning to the auctioneer, he raised his paddle with the number clearly visible and waited until the auctioneer wrote down the number. Maneuvering his way around God's anointed rancher to the center aisle, he strode past the bidders to the back of the room. As Billy was writing out his check to the cashier, the cashier tipped back in his chair, clasping his hands over his belly.

That was pretty smart how you knew about the initials. I read about em myself in *Billy the Kid: Outlaw or Hero*.

At the front of the room the auctioneer was already taking bids on the next item, an embroidered saddle from the James family.

Lot of errors in that book, Billy said to the cashier.

The female assistant came forward with the Winchester and whether because of the cost of the rifle or Billy's revealed identity, presented the rifle like a sacramental object. Billy turned the rifle over, checked for the initials and nodded his head.

The assistant gazed on him with smiling, hopeful eyes. Are you really Billy the Kid?

I was once, but am no longer, Billy said. Crooking the rifle in his arm like a man on a shooting party, he passed through the exit door.

~

Billy was back inside Peck's saloon, and the bucking bronco in the large cowboy painting was throwing the cowboy uncomfortably high, and as Billy observed the cowboy he had a feeling of vertigo. He shut his eyes and opened them again—and found the room reeling. Why he had drunk so much he couldn't remember. All he could do now was lean against the wooden post that had become his second spine. If he could have fumbled off his belt, he would have lashed himself to the post, but such intricacies of engineering were beyond him now. Once he had gathered his strength, he would make for the empty chair at the table across the room. But first he would get another drink at the bar. The bar. The bar, he now observed, had sailed like an argosy to a distant part of the room. He would never reach it now. His eyes widened as he observed the bartender turning his head toward the entrance. Stokes had flickered inside like a malicious spirit. From opposite sides Pawnee Broadfoot and Johnny Johnson approached him, and Johnny Johnson patted him down. An electric light on the wall lit Stokes's face at a garish angle, sinking his eyes into their sockets and lighting his front teeth.

The two Rough Riders allowed Stokes to pass, and he journeyed to the bar. Billy lowered his face to his hand, and when he looked up again, Stokes had an elbow on the counter and was taking out a cigar. The tip he bit off, spitting it on the floor and rolled the wet end in his mouth. In his hand was a compact device Billy had never seen before, and with this device Stokes lit his cigar. As if on wings, Billy's eyes flew across the room and read the inscription on the lighter—*Zippo*. Billy's eyes lost their focus, and the letters on the lighter bled dark red.

Stokes blew out three smoke rings from his cigar, and the rings spiraled up to the ceiling. On his face was an expression of infinite tedium. There was someone whispering in Billy's ear—it was his own voice and it was telling him the skylight, the skylight. Billy was lifting his head toward the ceiling when the skylight shattered. The falling glass fell slowly enough that he could make out the individual pieces. All around him were faces sliced and bleeding, and men and women crying out in separate voices that made a multiphonic chorus of their grief. More shattering of glass, and a large wooden crucifix came rifling through the opening of the skylight, but it wasn't a crucifix, it was a wooden coffin, and it was spinning, spinning.

The room was spinning. Billy covered his face with his hand again. He heard pounding footsteps and peeped out between two fingers. Johnny Johnson was sprinting toward the skylight, gun raised, but the faster he ran, the less ground he seemed to cover.

Billy dropped his hand from his face, and his eyes traveled up to the coffin. Peering from a slit in the lid were two glinting eyes. Another step from Johnny Johnson, and a cracking sound came from the coffin, and a hailstorm of bullets tore through the coffin lid. The bullets passed through air that was now a viscous fluid, and Billy could see the groupings of the bullets as they flew. In an instant Johnny Johnson crumpled to the floor, his blood coagulating in the dust.

In a ponderous length of time the bartender raised a shotgun from underneath the bar. Simultaneously Stokes let a pistol crawl from his sleeve to his hand, his finger making a slow tightening circle around the trigger, the bullet releasing with a muffled roar, and between the eyebrows of the bartender a red circle bloomed. Below the broken skylight the coffin swayed back and forth. The open lid revealed a drum-stick machine gun dandling like a baby in Plato's arms. From the far side of the room Pawnee Broadfoot was racing toward the coffin with raised pistols in his hands, but the floor was lengthening beneath his feet. Plato pointed his machine gun in Pawnee Broadfoot's direction, and from the muzzle that rose and fell there came a shaking orange flame.

Pawnee Broadfoot's arms stretched above his head as if he were getting ready for bed, and he took his last two steps, his tired legs stuttering under the weight of his body until they failed him altogether, and down to the floor he sank, the pistols in his hands letting out the last echoing protest of a man desperately trying to stay awake.

Everyone in the saloon was lying on the floor now, the living beside the dying.

Except for Billy. Except for Peck. Peck was taking languorous, high-bouncing steps in the direction of the coffin in a pointless and futile effort, and from his shoulder holster he drew his pistol. Stokes, lying behind a turned-over table, fired off a single shot, the bullet striking Peck in the back, and off his heels Peck lifted, extending his arms to embrace his dream one last time, soaring over the sandy planks with his ghost soaring beside him. Landing on the pillow of his stomach, he slid forward to a dreamless sleep, the back of his jacket leaking.

A scream traveled the length of the room.

The scream was a Mescalero death chant for fallen warriors. It was echoing now in Billy's ears, it was erupting now from Billy's throat. Bit by bit the room fell into darkness, and the scream died away in Billy's chest, and there was no more sound save his ratchety breath, his ratchety breath. In a sudden movement of his body he bolted upright against the headboard of an unfamiliar bed, his eyes wide open, his brow streaming.

He glanced at the wind-up clock on the nightstand in his Denver hotel room. It was 2:00 a.m. He stared intently at the clock until the minute-hand leaped forward. He was no longer dreaming. He had attended an auction in Denver, and he had had a bad dream, that was all. If he left Denver now, he would be back in Pueblo by dawn.

TWENTY-FIVE

As his car sped through the night, Billy thought about the dream that had foamed out of the sea of his fears, the dream that was not—could not—be a premonition. True, Peck's last words were about the impending fireworks, and it only made sense Billy's mind would latch onto those words. Because if the dream was a premonition, where were Stokes's chauffeur and doorman? And how believable was it that a coffin would lower through the skylight? But Billy would speak to Peck today, and he would tell him to board up the skylight, and he would tell him to never let Stokes enter the premises again. He would tell Peck these things, and he would make sure Peck listened to what he said.

~

Ten miles outside of Pueblo the sun mounted the horizon, and a long dark cloud became visible. At first Billy thought nothing of the cloud, but then he heard a clattering noise inside the cloud's dark center. The cloud cantered toward him as if it were alive, and with its approach the darkness of the cloud turned a dull green.

A hundred yards above the road the cloud hovered like an airship. The clattering stopped, there was a terrible silence, and an explosion rent the morning air. From the unpent sky came torrents of rain that fell through the air in pulpy green drops. The rain fell in such abundance that the air itself became glutinous and the earth a throbbing green fabric as far as the eye could reach. Billy smashed through the rain until his car emerged, streaked and bleeding, on the outskirts of Pueblo, the splash apron weighted down by five pounds of dead grasshopper.

The road to Peck's saloon was slippery. Stray grasshoppers were flying through the air, and Billy imagined he could see their hind wings snapping. Sluicing through the sludge, Billy brought his car to a sliding stop in front of Peck's Place. He got out, and as he strode toward the saloon, a sea of grasshoppers parted before him.

He paused before the entrance. One of the swinging doors was hanging from a single hinge. Billy entered the saloon and stared in mute horror. Grasshoppers were catapulting onto the bar and onto the scalp of the bartender who was slumped down in a corner, his head sagging to one side. The lidless coffin was there, dangling from the ragged hole of the skylight. Below the coffin lay Peck's lifeless body. Billy crossed over to the prostrate figure. Peck's tuxedo jacket was thick with dried blood. Crouching down, Billy rolled his friend over. Peck's lower jaw was canted at a ghoulish angle. On a hunch, Billy reached over and folded back the upper lip. Where gold and diamonds once sparkled, there now gaped a dark hole. Billy closed the lip and repositioned the jaw. From Peck's cheek he wiped away the sawdust. He had never touched his friend's cheek before. Tenderly he laid Peck's head back on the yellow plank.

Behind him he could hear grasshoppers bouncing off the tin chandeliers. He stood up. A few yards away lay Johnny Johnson and Pawnee Broadfoot, their clear brows untroubled now, their limbs outstretched as if they had been crawling along the floor like children until simple fatigue had overcome them. Billy turned and strode back toward the entrance. Inside him a strong emotion was welling up. He was fighting it down into his stomach, but it gorged up into his throat, and at the bar he turned and hammered his fist on the counter.

~

Billy was hammering to wake the dead on the front door of a house that was shaped like a rail car. The scurry of approaching footsteps, the grinding of the knob inside, and the door swung open. Behind the screen door a woman with frowzy hair was collecting her bathrobe around her waist.

Get Jack, Billy said.

The woman nodded and disappeared. Through the screen door Billy could hear a man grumbling in a half-awake voice. The voice took on a tone of urgent clarity, and Jack Warden, the sheriff, padded down the hallway in a nightshirt and slippers.

Billy, it's six-thirty in the morning.

Four men are dead, Billy said through the screen.

I know. Investigation starts this morning.

Billy banged through the screen door, grabbed the sheriff by the shoulders and slammed him against the wall. You know the men responsible. You're supposed to be the sheriff in this town, goddammit.

Investigation starts this morning, the sheriff said, his wide chin swamping his jaw.

Billy stared at him, grasshoppers grinding through the silence, released him and banged out the door.

Hey, the sheriff said through the screen door.

Billy halted in his stride and gave a backward glance.

If you're thinkin about revenge, the sheriff said.

Revenge?

If you're thinkin about it.

Revenge is for men who need to feel powerful.

So what you fixin to do, Billy?

Billy opened the door to his car and climbed inside. He started the car and rolled down the window. What I'm fixin to do? I'm fixin to stay alive.

TWENTY-SIX

illy carried the Winchester with him inside the Congress Hotel. The night clerk was still on his shift. He glanced up from his novel as Billy headed for the stairs. Eyeing the Winchester, the clerk said: What you aim to do, Billy?

I aim to get some sleep, Billy said.

In his room Billy stood the rifle in a corner and collapsed wretchedly on the mattress. His palm he placed over his chest. Anguish, he felt such anguish. He sharply regretted ever going to the auction. If he had been at the saloon, he could have done something, but with only his guitar what could he have done? The truth was he could have done nothing. He could have been a witness, nothing more. To think of Peck, Johnny Johnson and Pawnee Broadfoot fighting together in Cuba, and dying thirty-five years later on the floor of a saloon. The bullet striking Peck in the back—he shrank from contemplating it.

A movement under the bed alerted him, and he was on his feet in one bound, snatching up the Winchester. From underneath the bed Tommy wriggled out.

Got to learn how to knock, Tommy, Billy said. Almost got yourself killed.

Tommy rose to a sitting position on the floor. They want to shoot my Pa.

Explain.

They came to the trailer camp last night, lookin for him. You got to help me, Billy!

Where's your father now? Billy said, standing the Winchester against the wall.

Yesterday he went to Denver to get some supplies for Mr. Peck. When's he comin back?

He said around seven-thirty this morning.

Billy passed a weary hand across his forehead and glanced at the clock on his desk. It's almost seven now, he said.

Tommy sprang to his feet. That's why you got to help me, Billy.

I'm not a gunslinger, Tommy. I'm real sorry.

Tommy made for the door.

Where you goin? Billy said.

To save him, Tommy said, drawing a small pistol from his pocket.

Where'd you get that?

It's my Pa's.

Put it away, Tommy.

Tommy jammed the pistol back in his pocket.

Billy went to his closet. These men, how many were there?

You goin to help?

Billy glanced at Tommy. How many?

Four.

From the closet Billy took out a black frockcoat and slapped away the dust. What were they carryin, these men?

One of em had a figure-eight, Tommy said. Another, the one who shot the streetlamps, he carried a newspaper over something.

And there was a man who maybe had a gun up his sleeve. That was Mr. Stokes. And I couldn't tell with the last man.

One of Billy's arms got caught in the frockcoat as he was putting it on. Tommy jiggled out the sleeve until Billy's hand poked through. His mind deep in thought, Billy buffed his boots with the tail end of the bedspread.

You goin to shoot em? Tommy said, blinking his eyes excitedly.

Without answering, Billy crossed over to the Winchester and stuffed it inside his frockcoat. It was the first time Tommy had registered the existence of the rifle, and he couldn't contain himself.

That's lever-action, carries a dozen cartridges, uses a .44 caliber bullet, same bullets as your Colts, so all you need is one cartridge belt!

Billy opened the frockcoat and tore the auction tag from the rifle. You really know your guns, Tommy, he said, more affably than a moment before. Returning to the closet, he removed from a hook an old droop loop double holster gun belt.

You goin to gun em down? Tommy said.

Billy strapped the gun belt low on his hips and took down the gun case from the shelf in the closet. He opened the case and lifted out the two Colts. I'm goin to stay as far away from em as possible, Billy said.

One of the Colts would not fit properly in its holster. He gave it another shove, and this time he had success. We got to catch your Pa before he gets into town, Billy said, crossing to the door. He glanced at Tommy who was not moving. You're comin with me, Billy said.

As Billy and Tommy moved toward the stairs, Grace's door opened. Grace stepped into the hallway in a pink-flowered dressing gown, clutching the collar around her neck.

You hear what happened last night, Billy?

Billy paused in his steps before the staircase. I heard, Grace.

I'm just sick about it, she said. Her eyes alighted on Tommy.

This here is Tommy, Billy said. Stokes and his men want to kill Tommy's father.

His frockcoat opened, revealing his gun belt. Grace startled at the sight. You think you can face those men alone, Billy? You're crazy.

He is not, Tommy said. He's Billy the Kid!

This isn't some chapter in your book, Billy, Grace said. This is the real world. They'll kill you.

Hope not, Billy said. Still got a few pages left to write.

Come to my room for a moment, Grace said.

Have to go, Grace.

Come to my room, Billy, she said, turning to her room.

Billy drew a breath and walked toward her room. Behind him he could hear Tommy's footsteps keeping pace. Holding his arm out parallel to the floor, he turned to Tommy. Wait right here.

TWENTY-SEVEN

A preacher's voice was declaiming from the radio: And chief among our modern ills is the decline in church attendance. This is Reverend Fulton J. Sheen speaking to you from—

Grace snapped off the radio as Billy came inside the room. It was a room he hardly recognized. Gone were all the photographs of her husband—even the painting was missing. And hanging in its place was an unframed canvas of flaring reds and incandescent oranges. Billy stood before the canvas, and then came the dawning recognition. It was the slag.

Got your eye back, he said over his shoulder.

I thought you wrote your book to show how a man could change, came her voice.

Billy turned toward her. Grace was resting her hands on the back of her armchair.

I have changed.

How?

He stood there, expressively silent.

How? Grace said.

I'm about to help a man I don't even like.

Grace took two steps backward to block the door. Billy, don't go. I don't want you to go. Don't. Please.

Grace, they want to kill the boy's father.

But the sheriff and his deputies.

Won't lift a finger.

I can't go through this, Billy, not a second time.

Billy moved closer, so close he could draw her to his chest. The extraordinary thing about love was its rhythm. Love had its own rhythm, independent of the carefully calculated rhythm of our carefully calculated lives.

Billy lowered his gaze. I have to go, Grace.

When was the last time you fired a gun?

He glanced up at her. In a saloon, a few days ago. I was drunk.

When was the last time you fired a gun at a man?

He looked at her with lost eyes.

Wait right there, she said. She slipped past him and went into the bedroom, and when she came out, she had a package wrapped in brown paper.

It arrived two days after my husband died, Grace said.

Billy took the package and read the address label: Sheriff Patrick O'Bannion.

Open it, Grace said.

Tearing off the wrapping, Billy found a garment made of thick wire mesh.

They call it a bulletproof vest, Grace said. Try it on.

Billy took off his frock coat. With considerable effort he put on the vest and put his frock coat on over it.

Comes with a money-back guarantee, Grace said with a weak smile.

Worst case you get your money back, Billy said. He turned and went to the door.

Billy, Grace said in an aching voice.

His shoulders heaved. He would not, could not look at her.

She crossed over to where he was standing. What you're doin is noble, she said and pressed his hand in sympathy. The simplest touch of her hand was enough for him to reconsider his entire course of action. He pulled his hand away.

The more noble, the more foolhardy, Billy said, and strode past her into the hallway. At the staircase, he gave Tommy a nod, and not until they were halfway down the staircase did he hear Grace's door click shut.

TWENTY-EIGHT

ith grasshoppers flying up against his windshield, Billy passed a row of small square houses. He turned onto the main road, now shellacked a brownish-green, and brought the vehicle to a stop in front of the gun shop.

What are we here for? Tommy said from the passenger seat.

Life insurance, Billy said.

At the shop door Billy reached down and shook a rectangle of grasshoppers off the welcome mat, found the key underneath and let himself in. In under a minute he emerged with two boxes of cartridges. He jumped back in the car and peeled out to the road. Moments later they were parked on the dirt apron of the road that leads to Denver. And there they listened to the grasshoppers while waiting for a vehicle that might contain Frank.

Presently a Model A sped toward them with a green fungus growing on its radiator. From a hundred yards away Billy could tell the driver was not Frank. Next came a jalopy carrying a family of Okies. Soon after, a Nehi soda pop truck came barreling down the road at a fast clip. Tommy recognized his father first. At once Billy and Tommy got out of their car and crossed to the middle of the road, waving their arms.

The truck braked to a stop, and Frank shouted out the window at Tommy: What the hell you doin here?

We're here to save you, Pa!

The hell you are. I've got a delivery for Peck.

Billy opened the passenger door of the truck and Tommy swung up inside. Billy directed his voice to Frank: Drive to the trailer camp by the back road. Tommy will fill you in.

Ten minutes later the two vehicles were parked beside Frank's auto tent. Frank and Billy spoke to each other from the open windows of their cars with grasshoppers springing between their faces.

I don't get it, Frank said. Why would Stokes want to kill me?

It's like I told you before, Billy said. You ditched him for Peck, and that's called switchin sides. Now you get your car packed up, and you take yourself plumb out of the state.

Your friend Peck owed me some money, Frank said. First I'm goin to sell Stokes the booze in this truck, then I'm goin to ask him to hire me back.

You're out of your mind.

Well, my business if I am. So you best be on your way.

I suppose I should be. Oh, I almost forgot, Billy said, getting out of his car. He crossed thoughtfully over to the driver's side of Frank's truck, and grasshoppers sprang away from his boots.

What did you forget? Frank said through the open window.

This, Billy said. He hurled a right cross against Frank's chin, and Frank's head snapped to one side. Frank burst from the car and dove for Billy, tackling him to the ground. Frank threw two punches, but with Billy's fast reflexes not one of them connected. Frank was about to throw a third punch when his eyes rolled white into the back of his head, and he reeled backwards, unconscious.

Tommy was standing over his father, a frying pan in his hand.

He was goin to kill you, Billy. Will he be okay?

He'll be fine.

Together they carried Frank's limp body inside the auto tent and loaded him into the back of Frank's car. I'll drive both of you out of here, Billy said. Help me pack up.

From outside the auto tent there came a low murmuring sound. Billy went to the flap and peered out. Gliding toward them over a carpet of grasshoppers was the Stutz. Billy let the flap close and fixed Tommy with a look. Get in the car and keep down.

Leaving the tent, Billy crossed over to his car and stood beside it. The Stutz braked a few yards in front of him. First out was Plato, followed by the doorman and the chauffeur. Plato's fingers were wrapped around the walnut pistol grip of his tommy gun. From the doorman's hand dangled a sawed-off Browning automatic rifle. The chauffeur was palming the pistol from his wallet holster. When Stokes finally emerged from the Stutz, he took stock of the trailer camp with a slow turn of his head and lit his cigar with a Zippo lighter—it was the lighter from Billy's dream—and glanced over at Billy.

Well, well, well. If it ain't the fastest retired toothpuller gun-fighter in the state of Colorado, Look at you and your getup. Where you goin dressed like that? The Museum of the West?

Billy shifted his eyes to Plato, and Stokes turned his head to follow the line of Billy's gaze.

Plato was looking inside the window of the Nehi soda truck. Plato threw Stokes a glance, and shook his head no. Sucking on his cigar, Stokes turned toward the auto tent.

That's private property, Billy said in a loud voice.

Stokes exchanged a look with Plato and leveled his gaze at Billy. I got no quarrel with you, except your bad choice of friends. But they've passed to their reward so I'm not much bothered by them now. Shifting a pocket pistol from his coat sleeve to his hand, he turned again to the auto tent. Billy opened his legs into a wide stance and raised his voice again. I said that's private property.

Stokes turned around and brought his foot down softly upon the ground. A curious expression formed on his face when he saw Billy's granite pose. What you goin to do, shoot me? Stokes glanced at his friends. Get a load of this, boys, the toothpuller wants to shoot me.

The men nodded their heads, amused.

Stokes looked into Billy's face, and his eyes hardened perceptibly. The world receded behind the two men, until there was only Stokes and Billy, Billy and Stokes, alone, alert, alive.

Go ahead, toothpuller, shoot the bootlegger. I dare you. I dare you.

The air cracked as Billy fired his gun. Stokes's gun flipped out of his hand. Son of a bitch! Stokes said.

Plato responded with a withering fire, but Billy had already disappeared behind a trailer with a swirl of his black frockcoat, and all that remained was the falling smoke of his Colt. Stokes made a gesture to his men, and they fanned out.

Plato crossed to the first trailer and pressed his nose against the side-window. A white-haired woman with curlers in her hair glanced up from her quilting. Plato surveyed the room and finding nothing, grinned at the woman. The woman gazed at him, immobile, and summoned up a small scared smile.

The chauffeur was running past a row of trailers. From the corner of his eye he caught Billy's black frockcoat disappearing inside the largest trailer on the premises. The chauffeur approached the trailer and kicked open the door. He lowered his head and climbed inside. With the muzzle of his pistol he flipped open the cupboards under the sink. With the toe of his boot he opened a closet door. Moving into the back of the trailer, he screeched open the bedroom curtain. He glanced at the windows on either side. They were too small to crawl through. He turned around with an expression of bewilderment on his face.

Crouching down outside the trailer, Billy was observing the chauffeur's movements through a slit in the rear vent he had just crawled through. He stood, wiped his forehead with his sleeve, moved to another row of trailers and flattened himself against the back of the two-story house car. Dozens of grasshoppers swarmed his boots. From out of nowhere a grasshopper landed on the back of his hand and rasped its hind leg against its wing. How peaceful it looked. He had seen many grasshoppers in his life, but never really looked at one before. They were a marvel of elegant construction, so delicate, yet so full of hardihood. The grasshopper, as if aware of being observed, whisked into the air. Billy turned his head and listened for any footsteps. There was only the grinding of grasshoppers. Down a canyon of trailers a scream echoed, and the grinding stopped. Billy peered through a space between two trailers. The chauffeur was flailing his limbs and scratching madly at his chest. Stuffing his pistol in his waistband, the chauffeur tore off his jacket, his tie and his sodden shirt. From his chest hairs a grasshopper fell to the ground and leaped away. Bare-chested, but still wearing his peaked cap, the chauffeur drew the pistol from his waistband and resumed his search.

From Billy's left came a fast crunching sound. Someone was running in his direction. Swiftly Billy took cover behind the church trailer. The doorman glimpsed Billy's reflection in the windshield of a car and ran toward him, firing his Browning automatic. But Billy had already scudded away like a ghost, and the doorman only succeeded in pocking the side of the church.

In the same section of the trailer camp, Plato was intruding his jaw into the open window of a house trailer. Inside, a family of four was cowering. In the opposite window a swatch of Billy's frockcoat appeared. With great stealth Plato poked his tommy gun inside the window, but as he was doing so, the trigger guard scraped against the window frame. Billy ducked out of sight just as Plato fired over the cowering family, shattering the opposite window. The next moment Plato sprinted around the trailer, but Billy was nowhere to be seen.

Minutes passed. Billy was lowering himself from the top of a small trailer, his Colts in his hands, when behind him he heard the smooth voice of Stokes: Slowly, very slowly.

Billy let his feet touch the ground. His back was facing Stokes.

Some lucky shootin back there, Stokes said. Now drop your guns and turn around with your hands in the air.

Billy dropped his pistols, which were swarmed over with grasshoppers, and turned around, his hands in the air. Stokes had his pocket pistol trained on him.

Now the rifle, Stokes said.

Billy pulled out the Winchester from his frockcoat and lowered it to the ground, his eyes not leaving Stokes's face.

Now raise up your hands and step away from that trailer. I don't want to mess up the paint.

Billy raised his hands and stepped away from the trailer, his eyes traveling up the barrel of Stokes's pistol to Stokes's mouth.

I meant to ask, how are the teeth? Billy said.

With his free hand Stokes tested the firmness of his front teeth. Teeth are good, Stokes said. You should've stuck to dentistry. But speakin of teeth.

His fished into his pocket and produced a bloodied handkerchief that unfolded in his palm to reveal four gold teeth studded with diamonds. Blood was still clinging to their roots.

I've done dread deeds, Stokes said, but only because I had to. Your friend should have joined forces with me like I suggested. I had to collect the money that was owing from the business he took. Maybe I took one too many of these, he said, glancing at the teeth. But you can discuss that with him yourself in a moment.

Through the crook in Stokes's arm Billy could see the alarmed eyes of Tommy. Tommy was crouching down and aiming his father's gun. As Stokes released the safety, Billy raised his voice: Tommy, no.

For a split second Stokes hesitated. At the same time Billy heard a clicking sound behind him. He flung himself to the ground just as Plato let loose a round from his tommy gun, accidentally taking Stokes down. Reflexively, Stokes fired into Plato's chest. Plato's legs buckled, and he toppled face-first into a pool of grasshoppers.

Stokes, Plato and Billy lay on the ground together as grasshoppers enshrouded their bodies.

There was a steady grinding chorus in the air, and a figure stirred beneath the insects. Billy rose to his feet, his hands pouring off grasshoppers and gripping his two pistols.

Tommy rushed over with his gun. I was goin to kill him.

I know you were.

Why didn't you let me?

I didn't want you to have that feelin.

From behind a trailer appeared the doorman and the chauffeur, their guns at the ready. At the sight of the two bodies, the doorman's mouth fell open, and it was the first time Billy had a chance to see his teeth. They were stained.

It's all over, Billy said, holstering his guns. Go on home. Go on now. Go home.

In the distance the plaintive note of a siren was splitting the air. The doorman and the chauffeur looked at each other and dashed toward the Stutz. As the Stutz departed, the sheriff's car bumped down the lane and skidded to a stop before the day's defilement. Exiting the car, the sheriff stared at the dead bodies now wrapped in living green cerements. Hell of a town for an undertaker, he said. Climbing back into his car, he sped off. The siren bleated for a few more seconds and went dead.

~

Frank was packing the green tent into the trunk of his car with Tommy's assistance. Billy watched with his foot resting on the running board. Shutting the trunk, Frank turned to Billy.

Don't know how to thank you.

Buy my book when it comes out.

Your book?

My Life and Times, by Billy the Kid.

I'll look for it.

Where you headed?

Southern California if the car holds out, Frank said, moving around to the driver's door.

In case it don't, Billy said, reaching into his pocket and taking out an old Zuni money clip. Detaching several bills, he pressed them into Frank's hand.

Frank looked as if he was about to say something but changed his mind and got in the car and turned on the ignition. Billy went over to the passenger side and looked at Tommy.

Give me your hand, Tommy.

Tommy put his hand out the window as if to shake goodbye. Billy turned Tommy's hand around so the palm was facing up and slapped it with his pocketknife.

There's Yucca plants galore in Southern California, Billy said.

Tommy looked at the pocketknife, speechless.

Take care of yourself, Tommy.

As Frank's car passed a row of trailers, Tommy poked his head out the window and gazed at Billy. Billy held his gaze until the car left the trailer camp.

Billy was walking back to his car when a thin voice called out: Gunslinger.

Billy whirled around, drawing one of his Colts. Plato, not dead, but half-alive and leaning on his tommy gun for support, touched the trigger.

The bullets slammed into Billy's chest and left arm, which dropped the Colt from his hand. The bullets pushed him backwards in small hesitant steps, like a man politely excusing himself from a dance, until he sagged to his knees and fell sideways to the ground. At the same time Plato slumped dead, his eyes frozen on the forward sight of his weapon.

TWENTY-NINE

In a chair by the window sat Grace O'Bannion, eyes shut, fingers interlaced in her lap. There was the sound of a gun firing outside, and her eyes flew open. She turned her head to the window. A car was backfiring, nothing more. From the side table she picked up some knitting, put it in her lap and promptly put it back on the table.

She was cleaning out a cupboard in the kitchen when she heard two knocks on her door. With mounting trepidation she crossed to the door and opened it. The sheriff was standing in the hallway with a doleful countenance.

Sorry to disturb you, ma'am. It's concerning Billy.

The light of impossible hope sprang in Grace's eyes.

I'm afraid I have some bad news, the sheriff said. He paused, then: He was shot.

Grace took a shuddering breath.

There was a silence of lingering seconds. The sheriff coughed into his hand and spoke again. His left arm is torn up a bit, but Doc says it'll mend.

You mean he's alive?

Oh, yeah. And kickin.

Grace held onto the frame of the door to support herself.

Mrs. O'Bannion?

Thanks be to God.

I'd sure like to know where I could get my hands on what he was wearin.

Pardon me?

One of those vests, those bulletproof vests. Billy said it saved his life.

Yes, of course, Sheriff, Grace said, fixing her hair with one hand. I'd be happy to get that information for you tomorrow.

The sheriff tipped his hat. Thank you, ma'am. And sorry about the bad news.

∿

The two spitters were having a meeting on the rail of the Thatcher building when Billy traveled over in his car with Grace. She had shed her black mourning clothes and was now garbed in a dove grey suit and matching hat. Idling the engine, Billy hollered through the window that he was goin to miss the meeting. As he put the car in gear, he could hear the words of the spitters drift over the sound of the engine.

Think he's really Billy the Kid? the gun dealer said.

Is now, the bricklayer said.

Is now, the gun dealer said.

∿

An open field. Hanging from the heavens is a sun dog, a mock sun, refracting mocking light through a cumulonimbus to the left of the true sun. Billy rides into view in a suspended trot on Gabriel's new horse from Texas. The Mustang Paint has one blue eye and one brown eye, and each side of the horse's face tells a different story. With a practiced movement Billy draws two Colts from his holsters and twirls them in opposite directions. Thirty yards away Gabriel takes two silver dollars from his pocket and tosses them high into the air. Standing beside Gabriel is Grace with eyes stretched wide as she watches the twirling guns and tumbling coins.

Billy slips the horse into a canter. Both guns he fires at the coins in mid-descent. Grace claps her hands like a schoolgirl, her face flushed with happy hues, and one of her dimples winking. Billy holsters his guns and wheels the horse over to Grace, who is still clapping. With one fluid motion, he pulls her onto the back of the Paint, and together they ride off.

Gabriel rushes into the field to pick up the silver dollars from the ground. His eyes are full of hope. He finds the coins and turns them over in his hand. One of the coins is scored and bent from a bullet. The other is not. He examines the unbent coin and two vertical creases appear on his brow. As if to question whether Billy is El Chivato, whether Billy is Billy the Kid. He examines the bent coin and his brow smooths out into one horizontal line of certainty. As if to acknowledge Billy must be Billy the Kid, he must be, he must be...

Gabriel drops the unbent coin to the ground. He hurls the bent coin toward the sky where it disappears into the slanting beams of the sun, the true sun, the one true sun in the sky.

ABOUT THE AUTHOR

Peter Meech is a writer, director and producer in television and film. His memoir, *Mysteries of the Life Force: My Apprenticeship with a Chi Kung Master*, has been translated into several languages. He has an M.A. in Communications from Stanford, where he won a Stanford Nicholl writing award. He lives in Los Angeles.

Sentient Publications, LLC publishes nonfiction books on cultural creativity, experimental education, transformative spirituality, holistic health, new science, ecology, and other topics, approached from an integral viewpoint. We also publish fiction that aims to intrigue, stimulate, and entertain. Our authors are intensely interested in exploring the nature of life from fresh perspectives, addressing life's great questions, and fostering the full expression of the human potential. Sentient Publications' books arise from the spirit of inquiry and the richness of the inherent dialogue between writer and reader.

Our Culture Tools series is designed to give social catalyzers and cultural entrepreneurs the essential information, technology, and inspiration to forge a sustainable, creative, and compassionate world.

We are very interested in hearing from our readers. To direct suggestions or comments to us, or to be added to our mailing list, please contact:

SENTIENT PUBLICATIONS, LLC

PO Box 1851
Boulder, CO 80306
303-443-2188
contact@sentientpublications.com
www.sentientpublications.com